LOVE
comes
SOFTLY

...a romance collection...

LINDA RUTH BROOKS

GUM TREE press

A catalogue record for this book is available from the National Library of Australia

Fiction/romance/contemporary & historical romance

Cover, text design, typesetting & interior design by *Linda Ruth Brooks*
Photo artwork: *Linda Ruth Brooks*

ISBN: 978-1-7644921-0-2

Love Comes Softly, and other books by Linda Brooks may be purchased through online bookstores and retail outlets

Author

Linda Brooks lives in Adelaide. She writes nonfiction, poetry, fiction and short stories. She has published and illustrated children's books. She has a BA Hons in Creative Writing from Southern Cross University. She gained a publisher for her childhood memoir *A Curious & Inelegant Childhood*. She has written a nonfiction book on living with Asperger's Syndrome *I'm not broken, I'm just different* and the children's book *Callan the Chameleon* with contributions from Professor Tony Attwood.

Published in anthologies: 'Coastlines' 5, 6, 7 & 8 (Southern Cross University); 'Wood, Bricks & Stone'; 'Grieve', 'Third Wednesday Poets' and 'Longing for Solitude'. Awards: Rebecca Coyle Scholarship for Hons; first prize for The Legacy University Level Creative Writing Award; first prize in the Gabe Reynaud Creative Writing Award and the Mater Misericordiae Grieve Writing Award.

A registered nurse and advocate for disability in a previous life, Linda has a rich background in listening to the stories of others, never shying away from the darker, gritty tales. And yet, humour is never far away. Linda enjoys hearing from her readers (even if they've found typos):

lindaruthbrooks@bigpond.com

Author titles

Nonfiction:
I'm not broken, I'm just different
(on autism with Professor Tony Attwood)
A Curious and Inelegant Childhood

Poetry
The Long Acre Paddock
Verse

Fiction:
A broken hallelujah
Behind Whispering Hands
Butterfly Pinning
Prose
Scarlett doesn't live here anymore
The Lost stories of Lucy Meredith Carter
The Unprize
Under the Bracken Fern

Publisher of the anthologies:
We are Australian'
The Great Australian Shed
Waltzing Matilda

Children's books:

A Tabby Never Forgets

Callan the Chameleon (Autism Syndrome)

Dusty Bunny's Very Important Job

Izzy & Pudding the Cat

I want a monkey!

Madam Iris Bigglesworth

The Banyula Tales - 6 stories

Who Stole Christmas?

The Flame Tree
You glow golden red; then
leaf by negligent leaf
you flutter
back to Mother Earth.

The shelter of your vibrance,
your blood-red lace elegance
fades, then drifts softly down
abandoning me.

On crackling colourless carpet
I wander
in dreary dreams
alone, bereft.

Return to me soon
red splendid charm
and shelter me
once more.

Bring back your beauty to me
The transient bliss—drift gently
You belong, not to the earth,
But to me.

So briefly you were mine.

Contents

The flame tree

An icy southerly seeped under the French doors into the detached granny flat. The blue of the sky was obscured by dark threatening clouds. The day had started poorly and showed no sign of improving. At least the police had left, after taking copious notes; giving Leisa the all-clear to tidy the rooms.

Maybe things would get back to normal now. It wasn't every day a client died quietly on the floor at the *Belle Maison Bed & Breakfast*. Eleanor Mansfield had left the world that morning in the same way she had lived her latter days; without fuss or fanfare.

Earlier, the place had buzzed with activity; ambulance, police and the local doctor.

Then everyone had gone as quickly as they came, asking where the nearest take-away could be found. Except for Dr Grainger who was pleasantly ensconced at her kitchen table being waited on by two of her elderly clients, Sissy and Celia Fenn.

Leisa Reid wiped off the sweat that was streaming down her forehead with the back of a grimy hand. Her fine blonde hair was tied in a ponytail with a cleaning rag, making her look younger than her 27 years. Wisps of hair escaped, framing her dainty face. She knelt on the floor; scrubbing the timber boards distractedly.

The silence of the morning was broken by the rhythmic sounds of the scrubbing brush on timber, and the gentle scraping of the flame tree branches on the bay window.

On the love seat under the windows, Banjo the kitten, stealthily eyed his errant tail with the intensity of a lion cub stalking its prey, as it flicked across his line of vision. Leisa sighed. At least the cat had stopped tipping the rubbish bin over and chasing the papers around like a frantic one-man hockey team.

At times like these she wondered what had possessed her to turn her spacious home into a B&B. Three policemen, two ambulance men, two undertakers, a doctor and a body bag were too much for anyone before 8 am. At least the other guests were cosy inside the main house, separate from the drama that had interrupted Leisa's morning.

Looking at her watch, she realized it was nearly time to prepare lunch for her guests. She groaned as she struggled to her feet and rubbed her lower back. She only had to clean out the bedside table and the bedroom would be finished. Then she could try to figure out what to do with Eleanor Mansfield's meagre possessions.

She opened the top drawer. There was a small old fashioned biscuit tin with the lid beside it as if Eleanor had been looking at it moments ago. Leisa shivered. The room was cold. She would be glad to be rid of the sad pall this woman had worn like a shroud.

Feeling like an intruder she removed the tin. Inside was a

small key. There was also an envelope that had a photograph attached with an old metal paperclip. The photo was of a boy who looked no more than ten. The envelope was sealed and there was a name "Michael Randall" written in thick scrawl. The writing was unlike Eleanor's feathery script.

Only six months before, Eleanor Mansfield, Leisa's youngest resident, had come to Belle Maison with secrets; and she had died taking those secrets with her.

When Leisa and her father, James Reid, had first arrived in Sydney the house had seemed empty, but not for long. James turned one of the large upstairs rooms into an office, taken on a business partner and employed a live-in housekeeper, Estelle, a widow who declared that the outside granny flat suited her perfectly.

Estelle had married Richard, James' partner. When James Reid died ten years after moving in Richard and Estelle helped Leisa turn the rambling house into a thriving B&B. Her plans to run a catering business were put on hold. The situation had attracted older clients, initially needed temporary accommodation, however, they had stayed and formed part of a hodgepodge family.

Leisa currently had three guests, now that Eleanor Mansfield had died. Along with the Fenns, twin sisters who bickered constantly, there was a returned soldier, Tom Barwick, affectionately known as the Colonel, who delighted in mucking about in the garden and not having to fix his own meals.

After cleaning Eleanor Mansfield's room and packing her

belongings, Leisa spent the day divided between cooking and calming the anxious Fenn sisters, who shared a room at the front of the house. She was just cleaning up after the evening meal when she heard flying gravel.

Only her best friend, Chelsea, drove like that. She welcomed the distraction of Chelsea's visit. It would be good to get her opinion on her current dilemma about the dead woman's belongings.

'Oooh, I love a good mystery,' chirped Chelsea when Leisa had finished her tale.

Leisa sighed. 'I don't have your spirit of adventure, Chels, so far this 'mystery' has only caused me grief. I wish I knew what to do about this letter,' said Leisa, tapping the table more vehemently than she intended. She pointed at the letter as if it were poison.

'It's only a letter Leisa, really! It won't bite.'

'That's alright for you to say, you weren't the one to find a dead woman in one of your rooms, and then have to put up with the police asking questions.'

'You poor love, why didn't the police take the letter or any of her things?'

'I thought they would. But after interviewing me they only took her purse with her ID and money. I asked what happened next. They were so casual, they said, "It's a coroner's case now, love. There'll be an autopsy and a report but the doctor said there was no reason to think there was anything suspicious about her death". When I asked what to do with her things they said, "We're not some sort of lost property, love. We can't be responsible for every unclaimed piece of kip. Nothing for you to worry about. Just send it all to her next of kin". I mean really, two suitcases and bags of clothes. With no past or forwarding address. I felt stupid telling them she had refused to provide a next of kin.'

'What'd the cops say then?'

'I told them that she was an odd sort of woman, didn't mix with the others; called them old busy bodies. They said, if and when, they rounded up any family information someone would ring me. But then I found the letter and phoned the police station instead. I told them about the letter with the name, the photo and the key. I told them someone needed to come and take care of those. But they said that wasn't their problem. They had no trouble finding Eleanor's family as Mansfield was her maiden name. She had grown up in Sydney and her family live here.'

'Then they should have come up with something, surely,' said Chelsea.

'You'd think so, but her parents are both in a nursing home. The cops said an aunt and nephew of Eleanor's had been in to identify the body and asked about money. I overheard someone mutter in the background about a family scandal. But they could have been talking about anyone. Anyway, the cops were tight lipped; they just said she had been estranged from her family for some time and I should just donate her things to charity.'

'That's cold. Some people have sad lives.'

'Just as well I have my eccentric family,' said Leisa.

'That would be all well and good if you weren't using them to avoid relationships with men,' Chelsea said, scrutinizing

Leisa over the rim of her coffee cup.

'I'm not using them to avoid relationships,' said Leisa defiantly, 'I'm using them to replace relationships with men.'

'How's that working for you?' asked Chelsea with an assessing look.

'Very well, thanks for asking.' Leisa's lips pursed and she folded her arms defensively.

'I believe you. Thousands wouldn't.'

'Now you're just being sarcastic Chelsea, you know I can't trust anyone after Justin.'

'I know. I was there, remember.'

'Yes, and God knows what would have happened if you hadn't walked through the door when you did.'

'I would hazard a pretty good guess that Justin would have hit you. He already had his fist raised when I walked in.'

'I was so stupid. He was just after my money. He assumed I would sell the house and invest in his latest get rich scheme after dad died. How can I trust a man again? I can't even trust myself to pick the good from the bad. What sort of hope does that give me?'

'It gives you the best kind of hope. You're older and wiser. He was only one man, Leisa. You met him when you were vulnerable. But the best thing that gives you a good chance is that you are a truly fabulous human being.'

Leisa's eyes shone with unshed tears. 'You're just biased.'

'Rubbish! I'm the biggest cynic on the planet, 'Hard Case Prentiss' they call me. No, I'm just a woman of great discernment, and you Leisa Reid, are a gem.'

Blinking back tears, Leisa tore the cleaning rag from her

hair and went to the kitchen sink to wash her hands. Flicking her long straight blonde hair back she wiped her eyes and rejoined Chelsea at the table. Chelsea knew she had said enough for now, but one way or another she would encourage Leisa to stop living for her eccentric guests, and her gourmet cooking and start living again.

It wouldn't be easy; the next man to impress Leisa would have his work cut out for him. Chelsea knew that behind Leisa's fragile appearance was a woman of steel.

'I have to make some attempt to deliver that letter,' said Leisa, changing the subject.

'We need to …' Chelsea rummaged in her huge holdall and brought out a large yellow legal pad. 'Maybe the photo is of her son who she left to run away with another man.'

Leisa smiled at her friend's active imagination. She knew she could count on Chelsea to come up with a story or two.

'The only personal information she offered was that she was a widow.'

Leisa felt a pang for the boy in the picture, whoever he was. This whole episode was bringing back the sadness of losing her mother as a young child. She felt a connection to this fatherless boy, not just because of her own sense of loss but because she felt responsible to deliver the letter addressed to him.

'It's a real mystery then,' said Chelsea thoughtfully. 'But this isn't helping you. We should look at all the Randalls in the phone book and call them. Take notes. That would be a start. We could look names up on the internet. Let's see if we can at least deliver this letter to its rightful owner,' said Chelsea taking over the practical role for a change. 'But before we start looking, I'm starving, I came straight from work.'

'I'm sorry Chelsea. I should have thought of that. I've been so distracted. I'll put something in the microwave, right now.'

Chelsea eyed Leisa watchfully. 'I wonder if the key belongs with the letter. It doesn't look like a house key. It's too small.'

'It is probably just some old key to some dodgy old suitcase that has long gone to the rubbish tip and we are wasting our time looking at it,' said Leisa. 'I will just be glad to get rid of this letter. It is playing on my mind. Anyway, if I find the little boy or his family I might find the answers to the key as well.'

The two women pored over the telephone book. After several hours of phoning they were no nearer answers. They began by ringing the M. Randalls, then all the Randalls in the metropolitan area, noting down the responses as they went.

'Why couldn't the name be Radinisky or something like that?' moaned Chelsea when they took a break near eight o'clock. 'There are far too many Randalls in this directory.'

'We'll have to stop soon. We can't phone after nine o'clock, it's bad manners.'

At precisely eight fifty-two pm their search paid off. Leisa had just given her spiel to the recipient—'I am phoning to locate a Michael Randall who may have had a connection to an Eleanor Mansfield...'

'I believe you have found who you are looking for,' a gentle woman's voice answered. 'Who may I ask is calling?'

Leisa told the woman her name and the brief circumstances of Eleanor Mansfield's life and passing. She scribbled down the address of the woman on the phone—14 Chelmsford Court,

Shellharbour. A piece of the puzzle had fallen into place.

'What did she sound like?' quizzed Chelsea in excitement. 'What did she say?'

'She didn't say much at all really. But she didn't seem to think there was any mistake. She said she felt sure the photo was of her son. Her voice was cultured and calm. She seemed reserved.'

'You can't expect her to open up to a perfect stranger over the phone I guess,' Chelsea said reluctantly. She looked as if she thought this unknown woman was a poor sort indeed to keep such a mystery to herself.

'At least Shellharbour is only an hour south of Sydney. She said she could only see me between ten o'clock and midday. I guess she wants to be sure her son is at school. She probably doesn't want him upset. I'm glad she can see me tomorrow. I can't wait to deliver this; it's burning a hole in my conscience.'

Leisa looked at the photo of the boy. He was a robust beautiful child with the kind of ruddy complexion that comes from outdoor living. His hands were thrust in his pockets, and his chestnut hair was unruly.

'I just hope that this doesn't upset the little boy in the photo—he looks a real sweetie,' said Leisa softly.

If Michael Randall had ever been called a real sweetie, he could not remember it. Now at the age of 32 he was a master builder, owning and managing his building company Enduring Homes, a company that specialized in custom-built quality homes for those who could afford his expertise.

Mike was a craftsman. He'd inherited his father's ability to build beautiful homes. Marrick Randall's, ability to build beautiful houses. He had inherited little else from Marrick Randall, the man he hadn't seen for the past two decades.

His father had been a wealthy man and had sent regular money to his mother via his accountant. That accountant was James Reid of Turramurra, and now the man's daughter was going to show up with some ancient letter and a photograph. She was up to something. The connection was too close to be coincidental. She had to know about his father's fortune and was after money. A ploy to get near the family.

Even though he had only been ten when his father left he clearly remembered the scandal his father left behind. The newspapers had been full of the news of the man who had eloped with a sixteen year old girl. Mike's babysitter. Mike remembered the curvaceous girl who had giggled and watched cartoons with him. Eleanor Mansfield must have only been in her forties when she died. That was one passing he would not mourn. His family had suffered enough.

He had been taunted at his public school in the city and had been relieved when he and his mother had moved to the coastal town of Shellharbour to escape the publicity and the fallout. The town had offered a peaceful life for him and his mother. His mother had shielded him and resolutely refused interviews with newspaper and television journalists.

And now, he would shield his mother in spite of the fact that his mother had vehemently vetoed his presence at her meeting with some woman claiming to deliver a letter, a Ms Reid. Somehow, he would intercept her and find out what she was up to without letting her know who he was. Mike had tried unsuccessfully to talk his mother into moving closer to him in the city ever since her diagnosis with MS. At least she had accepted a live-in nurse and companion, the lovely Nancy, whom Mike would ensure was present when Ms Reid came to call.

On the phone, this Reid woman had said she housed elderly residents who needed transitional housing.

I'll bet she does, thought Mike. I'll just bet she takes care of wealthy old women, and their money.

Well, he didn't need Ms Reid's nose in his business. Marrick Randall's abandonment of the family had been abrupt and devastating. Mike could still remember the media storm that followed. He wanted nothing to do with anything his father had ever touched or known, especially anything Eleanor Mansfield had in her possession. It had been twenty years since he had seen Eleanor Mansfield when she had been his teenage babysitter and his father's lover. His father hadn't contacted him when he was alive and Mike certainly didn't want this letter addressed to him.

It was just as well he had been visiting his mother the night before. Otherwise, Mike would never have known of this stranger intruding into their lives. Although his mother had tried to hide her reaction from him as they sat in the living room of her small cottage, he knew that phone call just before nine o'clock had unsettled her. He had waited for her to confide in him. And waited.

The breeze ruffled the palm branches against the pillar of the back deck where they were enjoying a late supper. The phone had rung just before 9pm. His mother's voice had been calm and measured, but afterwards she'd stared at the horizon and plucked at a corner of her shawl, a tell-tale sign.

'That phone call. What was it about, Mum? It upset you. Why can't you talk to me about things?'

'Because you have the annoying tendency to take over, assuming that my mind is as weak as my body.'

Mike gripped his coffee cup. 'I'm just trying to protect you. I'm sorry. I know your mind is as sharp as ever, but I know you were affected by that phone call.'

'Okay. I'll get to the point. It was a woman enquiring about your father,' said Marcia Randall.

'My God, mother, why didn't you tell me? That's awful. Was she a journalist?' Mike leaned scraped his chair closer.

'No, she wasn't a journalist; and no, it's not awful. And I don't tell you things for the very obvious reason that you would react just as you did now.' Marcia folded her arms and gave Mike the eagle-eyed stare he remembered receiving as a child when he slunk in the house trying to hide something behind his back. 'Why do you always assume it was the media? They haven't bothered us in years.'

Marcia Randall threw a corner of a soft knitted shawl over her shoulder and leaned back into the recliner chair. The ocean breeze had exotic tones. The smell of salt air had always intoxicated her. She heard Nancy rattling around in the kitchen and chuckled.

'How do you know she wasn't a journalist? They'll tell you anything. Did she ask to see you? Have a little "chat"?' Mike folded his arms and was eyeing his mother with a raised eyebrow.

Marcia smiled. Her overprotective son never missed a beat. She realized why he'd made it in business. He was tough, and when fired up about anything, was an unstoppable force. The fact that he went full steam ahead even though she'd insulted him amused her greatly. She was so proud of him. Not that she would say that tonight! She would torment him a little. It would serve him right for treating her like weak dishwater.

'Well, yes, she is coming here tomorrow.'

Mike bent forward, running taut fingers through thick chestnut hair.

'You're kidding me, Mum! I can't believe you're allowing one of those vultures into our home! I'll put a stop to this. If you were living back in the city with me, I could keep an eye on these things. I know you said you never liked the glittering social you and dad lived, but it would be different living with me.'

'*Oh, quite!*' said Marcia, glaring with eyebrows raised, waiting for him to catch on. It didn't take long. Mike knew of old when his mother's fierce determination could not be challenged. He sat quietly, willing his protective anger to abate.

'All right, I'm sorry for reacting, okay, overreacting. If I promise to relax, will you tell me everything?'

'If you promise to leave tomorrow's meeting to me, I will tell you,' said Marcia, her eyes alight. It was times like this, sparring with her son that she enjoyed their relationship immensely.

However, the same could not be said for Mike, who sat in mutinous silence, but only for a few seconds. 'So, someone *is* coming tomorrow?' he said, with deliberate calm.

'Yes.'

Mike opened his mouth to lecture his mother, then pushed the words back. He would never get anywhere this way. He had to trust his mother. Even though their roles had reversed to a degree, he didn't want to take her dignity. The bottom line for Mike Randall was that he adored his mother. She was the one woman in his life that he lay down his life.

'Okay,' he said gently. 'Would you like to tell me about it, mother? Please.'

The muted light from the kitchen window fell on her face as she turned to her son. Her hair shone like silver. Her wavy hair was pure white. No traces of the original chestnut hues, so like her son's, remained.

'Eleanor Mansfield has died.' She held up a hand. 'Let me tell it all before you rush in, okay?'

Mike reached for her hand, dipping his lips to kiss her sun-spotted wrist.

'Okay.'

'The woman who phoned owns a B & B at Turramurra. She has long term clients, that sort of thing. Eleanor died suddenly there. Aortic aneurysm, the sort of thing that's always unexpected. The woman, Leisa, said Eleanor hadn't been there long. Kept to herself. She said she knew very little about Eleanor. She didn't seem to know anything about the scandal or your father.'

'She wouldn't, would she.'

'It's been over two decades, son. Why would anyone be interested now?'

'Everyone loves a mystery, Mum. There's no time limit. A millionaire businessman drops off the face of the earth, along with his fortune. The media will always want answers to that.'

'Sometimes there aren't answers, Mike.'

'So why did you agree to see this woman?'

'Apparently, Eleanor left some papers.' Marcia bit her lip. 'A letter actually. With your name on it, and a photograph of you, in a school uniform. It must have been taken just before your father left. This Leisa seemed genuinely perplexed about what to do with it. The police refused to take the Eleanor's possessions and she was stuck. She wanted to pass it on.'

'This all seems very suss to me. Did you check if she was genuine? Ask questions?'

'No, Mike. Unlike you, I prefer the wait and see approach. The past can't hurt us anymore. I wish you could see that.'

Mike drained his coffee. 'If the letter is for me I should be here.'

'No! Honestly, Mike. You have to trust me. She thinks Michael Randall is a ten year old schoolboy. I'm not a fool. I am being cautious. I wouldn't have told you if I thought…'

Mike stood. 'Okay, Mum. I feel like another cuppa. How about you?'

'No thanks. You know I don't drink too much at this hour. You've got a lot to learn about women.' Marcia frowned as her son headed for the kitchen. Mike was up to something. His calm acceptance didn't fool her. Had she been right to tell him? If he hadn't been present for the phone call, she wouldn't have told him anything until after the visit. Her son had an uncanny knack of turning up at the worst and best times.

She'd waited until he was calm because this conversation and visit also involved the teenage girl who had wreaked havoc on their lives. At least that was the way Mike saw things. Marcia had been well aware of Marrick's infidelities and laid the blame for the affair squarely at his door. The teenage Eleanor Mansfield had just been the catalyst in Marrick's fall from grace and consequent disappearance. She would know when her son finally moved on when he let go of the anger towards not only his father but also the girl he left with. She knew the situation still stung Mike in a way that it no longer affected her.

He had only been ten, with no understanding of his father's actions at the time, especially as Marrick had gone so swiftly and completely from their lives. After a time Marcia had come to accept her new life, and only felt lingering sorrow for her son's pain.

Mike couldn't sleep. After Nancy had taken his mother up to bed, Mike searched the kitchen. He could see no good coming from this visit. His curiosity was only partly satisfied when he found a notepad with his mother's neat script and the name 'Leisa Reid'.

This Leisa Reid was up to something. Marrick Randall had regularly money to his mother via his accountant. That accountant was James Reid. He'd lived in the northern suburbs, that much Mike knew. And now a woman was arriving from Sydney, with the same surname, supposedly bringing papers after all these years. The connection was too close to be coincidental. She had to know about his father's fortune and was after money. A ploy to get near the family.

Even though he had only been ten when his father had left he well remembered the scandal his father left behind. The newspapers had been full of the news of the man who had eloped with the teenager who had babysat him as a child.

He remembered the curvaceous girl who had giggled and watched cartoons with him. Eleanor Mansfield must have only been in her forties when she died. That was one passing he would not mourn. His family had suffered enough.

His mother had shielded him and resolutely refused interviews with newspaper and television journalists. And now he would shield her. He would stay. The woman would arrive in the morning. Somehow, he would arrange to meet her and find out what she was up to without giving away his identity. He would see Nancy and make sure she was present during this Ms Reid's call on his mother. And in spite of his mother's wishes, Mike would be right outside. He was not one to leave anything to chance.

Mike rose early, after only a few restless hours of sleep.

He leant on the verandah column that overlooked the early morning calm of the ocean. He never tired of the tang of the sea air. The wind scuttled across the sand whipping tiny swirls in its wake.

He could hear Nancy in the kitchen putting the kettle on. She would be helping his mother get up soon. He hadn't had a chance to talk to her last night after the phone call. He sauntered casually into the kitchen.

'Ah, Nance. If I employed you on my building sites there would never be another complaint about the coffee,' he said as he breathed in the delicious aroma.

'You'd be hard pressed to get me on a building site, Mike,' said Nancy chuckling. 'Especially in the big smoke, I'm a country girl, born and bred.'

'It's hardly the country here, Nance.'

'Well, whatever it is, it's my idea of heaven.' Nancy worked with smooth movements. Now in her late fifties, she still held the air of one accustomed to smooth organisation.

He sat to enjoy the steaming brew Nancy set in front of him.

'I take that back,' he said, sipping the dark liquid. 'You can run my whole office; you always anticipate what I want.'

'Better than you think probably…'Nancy leaned on the kitchen bench. 'And right now you want to involve me in some conspiracy concerning that phone call last night.'

'Nothing escapes your eagle eye.'

'No, that's what you pay me for,' she laughed, 'along with my superior nursing and coffee making skills, of course.' She paused, waiting. 'Of course, I may not agree to help you. Your mother's wishes come first. I remember you were quite definite about that in my interview.'

'You do have a good memory, Nance. That's what, a decade ago? Don't tell me, you probably know the months and days.'

'Of course. It's not every day a brash twenty-something young man interviews a woman who's run many a hostel with the interrogation skills of the Stasi.'

Mike cringed.

'My mother has a visitor this morning and I would like you to try to be present, if possible. I fear this woman is trying to make trouble from the past.'

'That may not be as easy as you wish,' said Nancy.

'Well, nearby will have to do, if needs be. I promised Mum I would leave before the woman arrived, but I will be watching from my truck across the road. I would prefer that you didn't inform my mother of that fact. That shouldn't be too hard. Mother always sees guests in the back sunroom.'

Nancy smiled at his formality. He must be quite something in business.

'You had better "leave" soon then,' she said with a wry smile.

Mike leant against his sleek gun-metal Ute, legs crossed at the ankles, looking more relaxed than he felt. An active man, he'd tired of sitting in the car and was on the far side of the truck trying to keep an eye on the front door of his mother's house.

With a strong work roughened hand he held the torn piece of paper that had been on his mother's sideboard, "Miss Leisa Reid—10 am-12". It was just after 10.00. He hoped the wretched woman wasn't intending to arrive near midday.

He hadn't even laid eyes on Miss Leisa Reid, and yet he'd had enough of her. She was probably a poxy old money-grabbing spinster who knew the family wealth as well as the scandal and smelled money, one way or another. The papers were probably bogus.

Pulling at the collar of his stiff white shirt he realized that even though summer was drawing to a close the heat of the day was causing a fine sheen of sweat to trickle down his muscled neck. He wondered if it had been a mistake to wear one of his charcoal suits. In a small back street in Shellharbour, he must look totally out of place. He cursed his ignorance. He never wore a suit on weekdays, preferring tough Khaki work clothes and hardhat of his trade. Only when he had a rare meeting with an upmarket client who wanted a visit in the city, did he don one of his dark suits. As a one-man operator he'd avoided the corporate world with its inherent board meetings—his father's world.

It surprised him that he was churning with anger because some woman had phoned his mother about some letter. One that had been in the care of his father's mistress. Would there be answers? Did he want them after all these years?

Instantly alert, he saw a local taxi arrive at his mother's house. *A taxi.* That would be right, she couldn't even afford a car. His lip curled in disgust. A young girl got out, turning to the driver with a generous smile.

This couldn't be Leisa Reid. The girl was slight, with the unconscious elegance of a gazelle. She was wearing a white summery dress and carrying a fringy hippy bag. She looked no older than a teenager. She couldn't have been any different to his imaginings if she'd tried. If she was a journalist, she was doing a damned good job of appearing otherwise. The girl tentatively consulted a piece of paper before walking up to this mother's door.

Anger throbbed at the back of his throat. This was the moment he had waited for but he realised that his wait had just begun. With a deep throated moan he got back into the truck and tried unsuccessfully to concentrate on his latest blueprint. He'd hoped that his mother would dispatch the woman quickly but after just over an hour he began to chafe at the time.

A movement of the front curtain caught his eye. It was Nancy. She made a sweeping gesture of her hand that told him their visitor had left by the back entrance, where the beach was accessible to all.

He swore under his breath, but then realising this could work in his favour, gunned the truck into action and headed for the public beach access at the end of the street - with no real forethought other than that this would give him a chance to observe the girl, undetected.

It shouldn't be so hard, he thought. After all, she thought he was a ten year old boy. Well, that suited him just fine. She wouldn't know what she was up against. Miss Leisa Reid thought she only had a disabled woman with a small boy to contend with, but she would find out that she was wrong.

Sitting at the picnic table five minutes later his intention didn't seem as clear. The soft zephyr breezes of late summer and the glinting of the gentle surf was working its usual magic. This was home to him.

His anger was waning. It didn't help that the devious Miss Leisa Reid was standing barefoot with her sandals tied to her handbag and was leaning forward chatting to a stout toddler who was describing his architectural plans for the sandcastle at their feet.

The child's mother was nearer the surf where she was anxiously watching a small sprite of a girl frolic in the froth at the edge of the water. The small group were the only occupants of the beach; besides Mike, who now began to feel he was sticking out like a sore thumb.

'Mischa, don't go too far!' called the woman to the little girl. 'Why don't you come and play with Brandon?'

'Don't be silly, Mummy, He's a baby. I'm too big to play with babies!' The tiny girl threw water into the air as if to emphasise this indisputable point.

'Well this is your last surf. We have to go soon. You can have an ice-cream—but only if you come when you're told.'

The woman shrugged towards Leisa Reid and smiled gratefully as Leisa returned to the boy, this time heeding his request for help. She bent down, filled the bucket with wet sand and showed him how to upend it to form a perfect tower. The toddler clapped enthusiastically and crowed with delight.

Mike snapped the newspaper he had bought at the nearby kiosk, holding it aloft so that he couldn't be seen. Shoving his sunglasses firmly onto his face he made every attempt to concentrate on the sports page. Minutes went by.

'Brandon don't!'

Mike looked up in shock. The voice was alarmingly near. It was the mother from the beach. He looked down and saw the cause of her anxiety. The toddler had a dripping ice-cream in one hand and a thorough grip of the hem of Mike's trousers in the other. Mike sat upright.

He was dismayed to see Leisa Reid standing next to the mother carrying the woman's beach bag as well as her own backpack. This woman must adopt people all over the place at random.

The red-faced mother swooped on the toddler and grabbed the ice-cream from his chubby hand. This had the effect of making the tot scream piteously and use his other free hand to take an even better grip of the trouser leg.

'Let go of the nice man's pants and you can have your ice-cream back, Brandon,' said the woman severely.

This concept seemed beyond the comprehension of the tiny boy as the only consequence was for him to increase his vocal capacity. Mike was appalled to look into the soft hazel eyes of Leisa Reid to find her grinning.

'Oh dear, I'm so sorry,' said the woman, continuing to grapple uselessly with the small Tarzan. Grabbing her nappy bag with blue monkeys on the outside the managed to find the Baby Wipes and started a serious assault on the problem. But just as she wrenched free one hand the tot used the other to transfer his grasp to Mike's other trouser leg.

'Brandon!'

'Stupid baby,' contributed his exasperated sister.

With a generous smile Leisa took the Baby Wipes. 'I'll sort this. You get your children to the car.'

Heaving a great sigh of relief and offering several other apologies the mother grabbed the tot's hands, hauled him aloft and carried him, still screaming to the car.

'Why did we have to bring him, Mummy? He's so embarrassing,' said the little girl. 'Can we leave him at home next time?'

Embarrassment was Mike Randall's own assessment of the situation, that is, until Leisa Reid dropped her backpack on the ground to better sponge his trousers and there in the midst of a melee of female handbag essentials was a yellow legal pad with page after page of handwritten notes…

Mike shrank back, belatedly realising his sunglasses were hanging from one ear and swinging across his face. This was not how he had envisioned his first attempt at domestic espionage.

Leisa Reid peeled with laughter, a full-bodied mellow sound that belied her dainty frame. She stood with arms crossed while he grabbed his sunglasses, folded them with belated dignity, placing them in his shirt pocket. He had dispensed with the suit jacket some time ago. It sat folded over the table next to the newspaper that was now in disarray.

Leisa pulled a wipe from the dispenser. She held it nonchalantly, with a teasing question wreathing a face that could only be described as beautiful. Her laughing eyes were as clear as a cloudless sky. And she was definitely not a girl.

Mike cleared his throat and was disgusted at the crowing noise that came out. Never had he felt so ill at ease. He was well accustomed to being in the company of beautiful women but usually on his own controlled terms. He couldn't remember when he'd last been the object of such humour, possible in his gauche teenage years.

'I only bite on request,' said Leisa, putting her hand forward to give him the wipe.

Mike was sure he blushed. He couldn't believe that he'd thought she was about to attend to his grubby trouser hems herself. Attempting to cover his embarrassment he accepted the wipe and then winced at the strange dripping wetness of the thing. He held it apart with disdain.

'Not accustomed to baby paraphernalia then, big guy?' Leisa posed with a smirk that told him she was vastly amused.

Mike turned his attention to swiping rather inadequately at his trouser leg, giving Leisa the chance to observe him. His hair was thick and curly and glowed like copper in the midday sun. Lips pursed in concentration, he continued his ineffective attempts to remove the sticky remnants of the tot's ice-cream.

He didn't need her assistance. She should leave but she was reluctant to walk away. Besides he seemed to be in a foul mood or was a bad-tempered git. She took a step back and bent to pick up the bag she'd abandoned to help the woman.

Then the copper haired hulk chose to look up and give her a stunning smile. Annoyed that he could shift gears so effortlessly, she narrowed her eyes.

'So, you're an expert with babies, yourself?' he asked, returning the smirk she'd given him earlier.

Leisa stiffened. 'Absolutely,' she said, after a millisecond. 'Have a houseful of them. Dozens in fact.'

'So, you adopt orphans?'

'Not at all,' she said sternly. 'I kidnap them. I was just in the middle of one here when you foiled my attempt.' Her eyes were alight.

Mike tensed. The wretched woman was mocking him.

'Oh, so I'm the unwitting rescuer. That's why the little fellow took to me. I wondered. Funny it's a bit hard to feel that way with sticky trouser hems.'

'Which poses the question as to why one would wear a suit to the beach. In Shellharbour.'

'Yes, well...' he began, hoping for inspiration. 'I've just been for a job interview. I grew up around here and after the interview... well, I couldn't resist the call of the sea.' He leaned back with a satisfied grin.

'So did you get it?'

'Get what?'

Leisa raised an eyebrow.

'Oh, the job, of course. Yes, I did in fact.'

'Good for you.' Leisa looked at her watch and threw the handbag strap over her shoulder.

Mike stood quickly. He had to keep her talking. He hadn't learned a thing.

'Name's Mike,' he said. His mind was in whirl, then he reached into his pocket and pulled out the business card of his part-time carpenter and long-time friend. 'Mike Crane,' he lied, handing her the card with the smile that usually had women melting in his arms.

'This says R. Crane.'

'Ah yes, well you know the good old Aussie tradition of using your second name. First name's Ralph; dreadful name. Sounds like a dog's name.'

Leisa waved the card with the merest hint of a smile. 'So you're a carpenter?'

'Yes,' he said coolly, glad to be telling the truth for a change. 'And what do you do when you're not kidnapping children?'

'I'm not sure I should tell you. We criminals have to keep a low profile.' She relented when she saw his suspicious glance. Opening her purse, she handed him a business card with a photo of a mansion-like residence with a limousine parked at the front and bore the words, "Belle Maison, Gourmet Bed & Breakfast, Leisa Reid, owner/proprietor".

'I'm Leisa,' she said, with a small reluctant sigh. She reached out a confident hand to shake his.

'Pleased to meet you Leisa Reid,' Mike's face glowed. This spy thing was a doddle. 'And is Leisa your first name? Or a replacement for some other hideous appellation?'

'No, it's just Leisa.' She laughed.

It was a warm sound that sparked an unexpected response in Mike. He held her hand a little longer than necessary. She flushed and gently withdrew it.

A light flickered in Mike's brain and an idea that seemed like a gift from the gods took hold of him. Adopting a professional stance and clearing his throat he began.

'I know this is completely out of the blue, but I am currently in need of accommodation.'

Leisa tensed and stepped back, beginning to shake her head.

'Please hear me out. Just while I find something suitable in Sydney. For the new job, you know. I have to start in two days.' He paused; then stepped back apologetically. 'I'm sorry; it just seemed an ideal solution. I can give you very good references. Of course, you may not have any vacant rooms. But being the end of the season; perhaps? … er, are you all right?'

Leisa had withdrawn; her eyes wide with terror, both hands pressed over the centre of her chest. Mike was stunned. What had he said to bring about that reaction?

Leisa's alarmed eyes were on the cloudy horizon, and an absent hand was brushing raindrops from her arm.

Lightning flashed. Thunder roared. Leisa put a hand to her throat, struggling to breathe. Thick, dark clouds boiled across the ocean. Still frozen to the spot Leisa whispered hoarsely, 'So sorry. Storms affect my heart. Tachycardia. Something to do with the electricity in the air.'

Rain fell in dense sheets. Mike reacted instantly.

'Don't worry; it's okay. I know about that. My friend's teenage daughter has just the same thing. Horrible feeling. A reaction to magnetic storms. There's a windbreak around here with a pull-down front awning. It's just behind that sand dune. Come with me.' Mike threw his coat around her shoulders and with an arm in the small of her back led at a run.

In a few short seconds they reached the shelter and Leisa huddled in a corner while Mike pulled the canvas front down securing it with practised hands. He went to Leisa's side and automatically reached for her hand. She resisted until she realised he was holding a watch and trying to take her pulse with all the professionalism of a nurse. She relaxed against him.

'Sure is galloping. 150. Is that usual?' he asked; his concern evident.

'Yes, sometimes it's been as high as 210.'

'Wow. What do you usually do?'

'Get in the middle of the house or under the bed.' She smiled wanly, attempting to hide her embarrassment. 'Sometimes even in a cupboard, anything that provides a barrier, really.' She shrugged.

'Well, that makes sense. Would anything large, a human body, for instance provide a barrier? My friend does that to his daughter. Seems to help.' He held both arms up in a gesture of innocence.

Leisa looked up into his eyes. There was neither invitation

nor rejection in her eyes. Mike hesitantly wrapped his arms around her and drew her into the warmth of his body.

She shivered. Mike pulled her closer and felt his own heart quicken. Must be contagious.

The storm ended as abruptly as it began. As with all summer storms the sun was shining, mocking the former chaos. The wind had died down to a moderate bluster.

Leisa retreated from him.

'Do you feel all right now?' asked Mike, breaking the awkward silence.

'I'm fine really. But thanks for that. That was a new strategy, but strangely effective.' There was a hint of colour in her cheeks and Mike was relieved to restore the camaraderie they'd shared.

'I'm sorry to pressure you about the room,' he said.

'It's just that I usually take elderly people. It doesn't mess with the generations.' She shrugged in apology. 'I started with a young crowd, and it was chaotic, and unpredictable. Then I just seemed to keep attracting an older crowd and it worked. I'm sorry to be indecisive but I've just had a death with one of my residents and it's flummoxed me a bit. I haven't thought ahead yet. I did have a young med student last year, but he worked long hours and had a dog. That's why I relented. Sounds silly but it was great because he was a serious bloke and the dog was companionship for the clients, and also great for security.'

'Oh well, that makes me perfect. I have a dog, and I will be working from daylight to dusk. My new job is very demanding. My boss has started a new apartment block, and I'll be working weekends sometimes too.'

'You have a dog?'

'Sure,' said Mike. Bob, his foreman, had a lovely Labrador on site the other day. Maybe he'd lend it to him. 'Love dogs. Just because I'm not very good with sticky toddlers, doesn't mean I'm a disaster with all creatures.' He rolled his eyes.

'All right,' said Leisa firmly. 'I'll send you an application and when you return it I'll contact your referees.'

Mike was gobsmacked. Never in his life had he been subjected to such scrutiny. Even his first bank loan had been easier. If he hadn't possessed such marvellous self-control he would have gaped. But instead, he smiled, a little too broadly. He, Mike Randall, was being put through more hoops than he remembered.

Leisa quickly phoned for a taxi, instantly regretting her decision. What had possessed her to agree to send him a form? She usually weighed things up for days, aggravating everyone she knew, especially Chelsea. She rubbed her forehead in frustration as soon as she was safely in the taxi.

'Headache Miss?' asked the driver, after she had given him instruction to take her to the railway station.

'No. Thanks for asking. Just a very strange day.'

Mike sat at the picnic table watching her go. His former confidence died a quick death. In the past hour he had stolen his best friend's identity, told more lies than a conman, invented a dog he now had to provide; but inarguably, worst of all he had *begged*. For a room he didn't want in a B & B that looked like some dodgy castle that was probably decaying at this minute when he owned a penthouse suite in the city.

And that was if high and mighty Ms Reid would have him.

He could always pull out of this nonsense. No harm, no foul.

A yellow page fluttered along the sand. He ran and grabbed it. The writing was appalling, loops and twists, words running over the top of others. Not … a memoir! Oh no, was the blasted woman writing his father's memoirs? A proposition infinitely worse than a newspaper article.

Bob Crane wandered in to get his job list for the day. The on-site office was more like a workshop than many of the city construction offices that were more geared for sales than production. But this day, it was littered with paint tins, painting paraphernalia, and carpet squares. Mike Randall, who was usually out on the construction site was sitting with his head in his hands on a plank that was precariously placed on two large paint tins.

'What's going on, Mike? Thought you'd be out on the job.' Bob dragged a chrome chair to the middle of the room.

He was a tall, rangy man. Fifty years in the trade had curved his spare frame. He wouldn't admit that arthritis, or any other infirmity had slowed his abilities. He'd been officially retired for several years but found that having a large shed to tinker in hadn't satisfied his need to feel useful and enjoy the camaraderie of the workmen. Besides, Mike was like a son. Had been since his mug father, Marrick Randall had thrown their family and business into chaos.

'Bob,' said Mike, 'I need to borrow something for a few

weeks.'

'Anything for you son,' said Bob, a grin splitting his work tanned face, 'What is it you need?'

'Your name, Bob. I need to borrow your name, mate.'

Bob laughed. 'Good grief. I am intrigued, Mike. What could you possibly want my name for?'

'Well, Bob. Thing is, I gave your business card to a woman. It's a long story.'

'Well, you'd better get to it then, mate. I'm on the clock. The boss is a tyrant you know.'

'You're retired, Bob.'

'Don't get smart with me, young Randall.' Bob scratched his beard, a thin straggly affair that he claimed made life easier. 'Something has you rattled. I've known you since I worked for your father and you wandered in begging for jobs. So spill.'

Mike scanned the room. 'Let's walk. The smell of that turps is making me sick. I had to let the painters use the room. All that rain. Those storms. It's a right bog out there.'

At the fence-line Bob stirred a gas burner into life and set the billy to boil. Mike released a long, slow sigh.

'That tart. That woman … she's, well, she's turned up dead. Eleanor Mansfield.'

'Oh. Right. I can see how that would put you in a spin. Dead hey? Gosh, she'd only be young. Wow. Just as well the boys are at another site. Looks like this is going to take a while. Sit.' Bob held his mug between both hands, sipped and nodded as Mike told him the story.

'And you suspect this Leisa Reid? Of what exactly?'

'I'm not sure. The B & B seems legit. I checked it out online.

But she's the daughter of James Reid, Dad's…'

'…accountant. I remember.'

'It's too much of a coincidence. Dad and his money go missing. This James Reid manages payments to Mum.'

'You knew about that?'

'I do now. I mean, I knew before but never thought of the details. I was too angry with Dad to go looking for answers. He was gone. School was hell. I was never allowed to forget that my father was the sleaze who took off with my babysitter. The media drove Mum and I nuts. We moved, and I didn't want to know anything about it.'

'And now you do?'

'I don't know. It felt weird, you know. Hearing that she'd died. I thought I'd feel nothing, but my brains scrambled.'

'And the letter?'

'Didn't read it. Don't want to. If he can't say something face to face what's the point?'

The buzz of a chainsaw from a nearby emergency crew made conversation impossible. The two men sipped their tea, dunking Scotch finger biscuits that dissolves in the hot liquid, and fell on the ground. A crowd of seagulls landed and squabbled over biscuit crumbs. Now that the storms had passed the streets were throbbing with cars. Two women in lycra gear, with ponytails bobbing jogged past with sleek prams that resembled racing cars, while the infants inside sucked on bottles, lulled by the movement.

'What's this about borrowing my name?'

'Oh, that.' Mike related the incident with Leisa Reid and his subterfuge, a story that had Bob laughing.

'Hey? How'd that nonsense go over?'

'Pretty good, I reckon. I mean, well, she did go quiet. But it was the perfect opportunity. If I stay at the B & B I should be able to get answers. I can't go as myself. Obviously.'

'Obviously. Jeez, Mike. When do you move in?'

'Well, that's the thing. That's where you come in. She wants references.'

Bob spat his tea. 'You're kidding me. What the hell kinda B & B asks for references?'

'It's more like a rental, I guess. She usually only takes in elderly clients apparently. It'll be a cinch, Bob. If she calls, and I doubt she will, just tell her what a great guy I am.'

'You mean, what a great guy R for Ralph Crane, aka Mike, is?'

'You're making this sound ridiculous.'

'Oh, mate, I'm not the one making this ridiculous. I don't know why you don't just hire a private investigator.'

Mike opened and closed his mouth. 'There's a good reason I didn't go down that path,' he said, 'I can't think of it right at this moment, but … there was opportunity staring me in the face, and… well, I'll probably only be there a few days.'

'If she accepts you.' 'Honestly, Mike.'

'Um, there's just one more thing, Bob. I … er, told her I had a dog. She was baulking at having another resident, and well…'

'No. No, no, no. You're not borrowing my dog. I have more respect my pooch than to let you take her. You'd kill her. You know nothing about looking after a dog.' Bob tipped the remainder of his tea on the ground, startling the gulls. 'I'm going to love this!'

Leisa stepped out of the taxi. The panic attack at the beach due to her sensitivity to the electrical energy of a storm had left her exhausted. It was a long time since she'd been outdoors in a storm and experienced the racing pulse, shortness of breath and fear that these symptoms created. She usually found an inner room, with soothing music where she could lie down and breathe slowly.

It was good to be back at the B&B. As for Mike the tradie, she had second thoughts, hoping he wouldn't call in for an application. If he did, she would put him off. His smile had been forced, his demeanour odd, and that suit!

She took off her headscarf and wiped her face. This heat. It had been so inconvenient to lend the van to Chelsea, but she'd made the arrangement weeks ago for Chelsea and the woman at Shellharbour seemed adamant about the day and time. At least that was something out of the too hard basket that had been done. That letter had been burning a hole in her purse.

Hearing loud voices at the back of the house, Leisa hurried around the corner.

Former Colonel, Thomas "Tom" Barwick, leant on his walking cane, wobbling with rage that was partly fuelled by his current state of helplessness. He'd been attempting to converse with a mountain of man who seemed to speak only Pig Latin interspersed with a series of grunts. He wore a muscle shirt and his meaty arms were covered in bold, bright tattoos. A hairy belly protruded when he raised his arms to punctuate his words. 'Meeaunt sented me. S'all bout me aunt'elly.'

'There's nothing wrong with the telly,' said Cissy Fenn, whose afternoon siesta had been interrupted by the two men.

Tom's cane tap-tapped the stone courtyard of the B&B. this staccato tapping was due to his advanced age and the early signs of Parkinson's. 'You will have to come back when the owner is here,' Tom said to the mountain with slow deliberate enunciation. He thumped the cane on the stones to emphasise the seriousness of his intent and to stop the nervous tapping.

Celia Fenn, twin sister of Cissy, leant out of the French doors, took in the crisis and returned with a small frying pan.

'Celia! What are you thinking?' asked her shocked sister.

'I was quite good at discus in my time,' said Celia, brandishing the pan in what she considered to me a menacing manner. 'Could've gone to the Olympics.'

At the back of the house Leisa encountered Colonel Tom whose bushy eyebrows were bristling as he rolled his eyes at her. Celia Fenn was holding a frypan and Cissy Fenn was attempting to use the mobile phone her nephew had given her for her birthday.

Tom tilted his head meaningfully and as Leisa followed his gaze she saw a huge man lying on one of the deck chairs, one leg trailing the ground as he snored like a rusty chainsaw.

Leisa felt fear claw at her throat. Memories of Justin, her previous fiancé surfaced. The sudden blows that landed. The shock and confusion.

Walking softly to Tom she fought the urge to run. She had others to care for now. Frail elderly residents. Tom shrugged when Leisa whispered, 'what's he here for?'

This faint sound woke the mountain, who wiped sleep-dribble from his chin then curled himself into a standing position with slow ponderous movements that were all the more ominous for their lack of speed.

'What do you want young, er, Mister?' barked Tom in the manner that once had his underlings in the army quivering. However, this calculated manoeuvre had the effect of shifting his centre of gravity in an alarming and unexpected way. He grasped the table behind him and sighed.

'Aint 'ere to ruff nobody up,' said the mountain, holding up his meaty fists.

Leisa flinched. People who claimed they had no intention of violence were usually the very people who carried out acts of violence. She controlled her breathing and took a step forward, grasping the backpack in a death grip.

'Have you an answer, sir?' she asked with forced calm. A strategy she'd learned.

'Meema sendted me. S'all bout me auntelly.' The man's voice was a low menacing growl. 'Want what's ours.'

'He keeps banging on about the telly,' said Cissy Fenn still tapping at her phone.

'I see,' said Leisa.

'The one what karked it 'ere.' The mountain rubbed a huge thigh vigorously and shuffled away from the deck chair, but to Leisa's relief, he came no closer.

'So, Eleanor Mansfield was your aunt?' said Leisa in a tone designed to calm small children.

'That's the one,' said the mountain with some excitement at finally being understood. The smile should have consoled his audience, but the state of his teeth dimmed the effect.

'Ma sendted me 'ere. Fer answers. Y'know. Like, where's her

stuff? Like, yknow. Perssessions and stuff.'

'I see,' said Leisa, 'what's your name, sir…?'

The mountain straightened to his full height and said, 'Myron. Me ma is auntelly's sister, like.'

'I see,' said Leisa.

The Fenn sisters who understood nothing of the exchange gave each other a frustrated look.

'You'll have to see the police about that.' Leisa's voice cracked.

'Aint 'ere to ruff nobody up, but … I'm here to get what's due. I aint muckin' 'round, y'hear me?' He stood and moved away from the outdoor table. Leisa saw a knife protruding from a sheath strapped to his thigh and gasped. Her breathing became shallow and faster as the man approached, waving his arms and muttering incoherently. Bloodshot eyes looked her up down. 'Who's the boss 'here? Wass yer name? Yer makin me angry, lady, and I don't take too well to…'

The mountain's speech was interrupted by the growl of an engine and the grinding sound of clashing metal.

A black 4WD came around the corner with a bicycle stuck under its front fender.

The mountain let out a cry of primal pain.

'Who's the idiot who left a bike in the middle of the driveway?' said a gruff male voice.

The shadow of a man fell across the patio as Mike aka Randall/Crane came around the corner with a large dog on a leash. He had parked on the verge of the road, planning a calm, leisurely entrance but when walking across the lawn he'd heard a loud angry voice, taken in the threat, gone back and made an altogether more dramatic entrance.

Mike yanked the bike off the car, lifted the mangled thing up and asked the mountain, 'This yours, Sunshine?'

Myron the mountain swore roundly but took the bike and legged it down the driveway.

Leisa, shocked by the sudden capitulation of the visitor, treated Mike to her most welcoming smile and wondered where she left the application papers.

When Chelsea arrived with the B&B van, the residents, including Mike, were sitting around the huge dining table enjoying Irish coffee and Leisa's muffins.

Mike made room for Chelsea at the table, but Chelsea crossed the room and picked up the backpack.

'Jeez Leisa, what'd you do with my backpack? It's full of sand. Oh no! All my papers are jumbled. I'll have to rewrite the article for the preschool.'

Mike choked on his muffin. He had been eyeing that backpack as if it was radioactive, surmising that it held the secrets of Leisa Reid's intentions and deceptions, but he now realised that the blasted thing didn't even belong to Leisa; didn't contain notes on his missing father, but some scribbled pages by her friend Chelsea.

Having spent a lifetime trying to avoid the chaos left behind by his father, Mike was not enjoying the roller coaster that his life had become.

The only area where Mike had any luck was with the dog, Irish. A wolfhound with regal bearing, the dog was a gem. She was gentle and calm. She'd taken to his mother immediately, picking up the remote when she'd struggled to reach it. It had taken Mike all his time to get the dog to leave her and come with him.

Irish had been a care-companion, and this was obvious. Mike had trawled several pounds and animal welfare facilities.

Chelsea complained that they'd only left her two muffins. Leisa produced another batch from the huge oven. The two women talked over the top of each other in a way that confused Mike but they managed to keep several themes alive as they chatted with much laughter in between.

'Those muffins aren't out of your quota for the shop run, are they?' asked Chelsea. 'I'd hate to be the cause of you cooking until the early hours to make up for it.'

'No, no, I made extra.'

'For all of us,' trilled the Fenn sisters.

'I don't know why you do it, Leisa. You could sit around a pool in some exotic location, travelling for the rest of your life, but you choose this—madhouse.'

'We win,' said Celia Fenn, who was clearly enjoying the liberal medicinal enhancement of the Irish Coffees.

'Here, here,' said Tom.

Mike had never seen the like, the spontaneity, the playfulness. In fact, he couldn't remember sitting around kitchen table with anyone but his mother and Nancy, her carer. It was certainly something he'd never experienced with any of the women he'd casually dated.

The women in his life were carefully chosen for their decorum, style and independence. Any date with a tendency to cling or pry was quickly rejected. And now, here he sat with a cacophony of chatter with everyone freely sharing their reaction to the day's events with the Colonel in the mix, yakking as much as the women.

There had been anxiety and frayed nerves after the confrontation with Myron the Mountain. Leisa had deftly steered the conversation to lighter moments and the bounty of having Mike's intervention in the affair. Mike was roundly toasted with Irish Coffee, welcomed and given the application form, which was a lot less complicated than he expected. Sitting among the residents and Leisa and Chelsea, Mike felt that he was part of something, something tribal, something near to belonging in a group.

The Colonel seemed particularly thrilled to have another male in the house. He offered to give Mike a tour of the place even though it was dark outside and he was tipsy. He leaned on Mike's arm and talked nonstop as they walked around the grounds and the downstairs rooms while Leisa and Chelsea cleaned up.

This gave Mike a unique chance to ask questions.

'The van … is that a bus for the residents?' he asked.

'Sometimes. But it's mainly for Leisa's gourmet deliveries to cafés and restaurants. She's hoping to start a private catering service. She's done small events here and there … ooops, mind that rock, young man. It's a godsend you are, Mike Crane, surely it is.'

Mike mumbled and swallowed hard. He had clearly misunderstood nearly everything so far and the lie of his identity clawed at his stomach. He saw beautifully crafted rooms with high end finishes, stylish, plump lounges, glowing fireplaces.

At the end of the ramble, he escorted the Colonel to his room, refused the whiskey offered with the excuse that he needed to settle the dog Irish, Mike wandered back to the kitchen. Leisa and Chelsea had left, but he heard murmured laughter coming from upstairs. He couldn't tell if it was the women or a television, but he was reluctant to interrupt. Suddenly unsure of himself, he wondered where he would be staying, all the rooms seemed occupied, apart from the room where Eleanor Mansfield had died and he didn't fancy sleeping there.

There was a sign on a door leading off the kitchen. Mike had thought it was a pantry, but a white square of paper bore the words MIKE'S ROOM. It had been signed by the residents. There was a smudgy lipstick mark by Celia Fenn and a cross-eyed cartoon labelled MY HERO.

The single bed inside the small room was a shock after his king size bed, and more than once Mike found himself on the floor. At 1:00 am Mike gave up on sleep as he finally allowed the huge wolfhound to climb onto the creaking bed with him. He received an enthusiastic licking for his generosity, and sighed.

He took inventory of what he'd learned and had to admit that Leisa Reid was seriously wealthy, was a fabulous cook, did not scrawl copious notes on legal pads and treated her guests like family. And yet, he'd been given a tiny room with a dodgy bed and a large towel thrown on the floor for the dog. Not knowing what to think of all that he finally fell asleep at 5am only to wake an hour later to banging noises in the kitchen.

Clearly this Leisa Reid was a workaholic and not nearly as impressed with him as the rest of the house.

Mike left without a word, wondering how long he could last with the meagre room in spite of superior meals. Perhaps he could put the mattress straight on the floor to avoid falling.

When Mike arrived back at the house after an exhausting day where he could hardly stay awake Leisa greeted him with a cheery wave, a list of chores that involved emptying the room where Eleanor Mansfield had died. There they discovered yet another heavy battered suitcase. One of the latches was broken and the contents peeked through the crack.

Leisa set the room up with bed linens, towels and flowers while Mike gathered his belongings. Apparently staying in that room was non-negotiable, but after the shenanigans of the previous night he was grateful.

In the morning, Leisa sat calmly at the kitchen table staring at her laptop when Mike entered. 'Sit,' she said, gesturing a chair opposite at the table. Mike cleared his throat. He sat, folding and unfolding the top of the paper bag with the lunch Leisa had prepared.

Leisa looked up, but not at Mike. She was murmuring.

'Um, I wonder if that big thug will come back?'

'I reckon he'll be back. He said "we" an awful lot,' Mike leaned forward, haunted by his own thoughts. Would any of them recognise him? Should he intervene like before?

'They can't do anything,' Leisa said slowly. 'Why should I care? After all, they didn't want the woman while she lived, and now that she's dead… pfft.'

Mike was surprised by Leisa's state of calm detachment. He was accustomed to women who were reactive, brittle women with stormy eyes, jealous glares and high-heel tapping exits and entrances, daring anyone to ignore them and their sharp words. Bringing confrontations he avoided at all costs. All confrontations. All his life. He'd learned to take his mind to another place when lectured by teachers and school principals, women, and yes, even his mother. But this was different.

'I didn't want to move to the city.' Leisa's voice was soft.

Mike tensed, sensing nostalgia. He didn't like secrets, emotions and other sticky subjects. But…

'I came because of a tree, the flame tree.' Leisa said.

Mike sighed and shoved his frenetic thoughts aside. Leisa seemed in an odd mood, holding his gaze quizzically. What was on her mind…

'The flame tree.'

Leisa began the story. Her voice was sure and focused.

'Fifteen years ago, after Mum died, Dad and I left our country property in Tamworth to live here, in Turramurra. He was an accountant and when he was offered a position with a prestigious accounting firm he jumped at the chance. He could work from home, giving him more time with me. He couldn't face the house he shared with Mum, but I felt torn from everything familiar and from my mother.'

Leisa took Mike into the past. He didn't know why he followed her, but the tenderness of her reminiscences was steeped in the sacredness of sharing. Ground that Mike would not have dared to step on, but was being trusted to hold. A shiver sent goosebumps up his arms.

'When I first saw the large two-storey house with its abundance of shrubbery, I hated it. Why did we have to leave our farm with its little country cottage and the flower filled gardens my mother lovingly tended? After living in a country town with space to move, these city houses seemed practically on top of each other. And trains! Would I ever get used to going everywhere by train? I'm afraid I sulked fiercely, with shuffling feet through the viewing of the house. It brought the reality of the loss of my mother.'

Mike was caught, trapped in the story. His own anger and sorrow seemed part of Leisa's story. A story that had never been spoken in words, or shared with such tender honesty.

Leisa relived the day her mother told her of the cancer that was ravaging her body. At 12, Leisa had taken the news badly. They were sitting on their favourite wrought iron bench seat; under the vibrant flame tree.

'I didn't want to like this house, but when we walked down the limestone steps into the courtyard at the back of the house I stood still as a statue. There at the end of the courtyard, amidst the wild shrubbery, was a flame tree. And under the flame tree were several rough-hewn benches.

'We'll take it,' I said.

Dad just shrugged his shoulders at the real estate agent.

'That was sudden, Sweat Pea.'

'Mummy's here,' I said.

'And that was that. We had a home.'

Mike swallowed a lump that had formed in his throat. A compelling urge to stay fought with the temptation to leave, to run, to escape, that time honoured family tradition of silence. His eyes were damp with tears. He didn't want to speak, but he must, he must. His voice was rough with emotion.

'I'm Mike Randall,' he said, 'I'm … I'm not…'

'I know,' said Leisa as she slowly turned her laptop towards him, where the society pages had numerous photos of Michael James Randall.

'I'm so sorry.' Mike bowed his head. 'I hope you can forgive me for all the subterfuge.'

Leisa snorted. 'The patently obvious deception? Yes, well, it is reassuring to realise that you're a poor liar. Mind you, if you hadn't come clean I was going to evict you posthaste.'

'I don't blame you. Was it the dog that gave me away?'

'That, and the fact that I had time to research you after you arrived. Your friend, the real Mr R Crane was most helpful…'

'Should have known. He said he wouldn't lie for me. Or lend me his dog.'

'What were you thinking?'

'I thought you were after money or a sensational story.'

'You might have to expand on that, Mike Randall.'

As a southerly breeze stole its way into the kitchen, Michael James Randall told his story. The story he'd always thought of as his father's story, anyone's story but his own. The lost boy who'd been expected to stop loving his father because of the man's public transgression and downfall. The vulnerable child who only heard his father's name as a disgrace.

'Did your father … speak to you, er, before he left?'

'No. I found that unforgiveable,' Mike tensed.

'It seems … from my "research" that the papers outed your father. I read about the media frenzy when he left so I do understand your mistrust, Mike.'

Their murmured voices filled the void in the kitchen.

Leisa's foot collided with a heavy object under the table. 'Oh dear,' she said, 'I've got Eleanor's suitcase. The one I found under her bed.'

The suitcase was brought out and dumped on the kitchen table where Leisa insisted on sorting it into piles.

Clothes of various sizes; dank and musty, boiled lollies in glass jars, a dozen lipsticks; smeared and greasy and receipts for trains, movies, museums and zoos. The case was lined with old newspapers that Leisa folded and put aside to organise later in order of date. Underneath the newspapers was a small book, the sort of diary a teenager might have—covered with stickers and ribbons. A card was used as a bookmark.

'It's a business card,' Leisa said, flicking it over. 'It's my father's business card. That's so odd. Why would Eleanor Mansfield have Dad's business card?'

'What business would that woman have with your dad? Would it be with his accountancy firm?' Mike stared at the card. 'Maybe she didn't. Maybe my father did.' He felt a cold shiver build in his spine. Would the mention of his father always feel like this?'

'Oh.' Leisa turned to Mike. 'I hadn't thought.'

'And that might mean that Eleanor Mansfield chose this B&B for a reason.' Leisa turned the card over. The word "Accountant" was written on the back. 'Pfft,' she said, 'well, that's not much help.'

'That's my father's handwriting.' Mike's voice was solemn. 'Leisa. This is getting too complicated.' Mike asked.

Leisa placed a hand on his shoulder. 'What was in the letter?'

'I haven't read it. I was angry. I wouldn't even open the drawer where Mum put it. I think that upset her. But … it's probably time.'

'Past time I'd say. There seems to be a reason why Eleanor came here. I think she had a connection with my father as your father's accountant. She might have been expecting to see Dad here, for whatever reason. We at least know that she was no longer with your father. From all appearances here, she had been alone for some time.'

'That means … we, I still don't know anything about my dad. Eleanor might have come here after my father's money.'

'I found her upstairs on one occasion. She claimed to be lost, I made it clear that upstairs was out of bounds to residents. I mean that's where Dad had his office but any current client files are with his business partner, Richard.' Leisa closed her laptop. 'If you're interested, I think a thorough look at Dad's closed files might be helpful. There might be nothing there. It depends whether your father is a current or past client.'

'I would be profoundly grateful, Leisa.'

'No time like the present, Mike. Come.' Leisa stood and headed for the staircase that led to the upper rooms.

'Jeez, your father was organized,' Mike said, as Leisa opened a filing cabinet.

Leisa's father had a card system with a reference number for each client with minimal information: address and contact details. There were also file drawers for invoices, bank details, payment and investment information.

The card drawer was dusty. There was no card file for Eleanor Mansfield but there was one for Marrick Randall.

Leisa's hands shook as she handed the worn card to Mike.

Mike slumped into a chair. The last known address for his father was in Cairo. Searching for a more comprehensive file on his father proved fruitless.

'Richard must have the expanded notes,' said Leisa.

'That would mean that my father might be a current client. He might still be alive.' Mike had just given voice to his deepest suppressed musings. After claiming that he didn't care where his father was, or what happened to him, Mike realised that was a lie. He wanted to know.'

In a brief phone call to Richard, her father's accounting partner, Leisa arranged an appointment for them to see him. 3pm later that day.

'I didn't think I cared,' Mike said. Three o'clock seems far away. I should go to work and keep busy.'

'You sure, Mike. You've had quite a shock. You could go to Shellharbour and make it back here in time...'

'The letter.' Mike paced the kitchen.

'If you're half as curious as I am...' said Leisa.

Mike looked at her with new eyes, bright with excitement. 'Come with me. The beach is lovely and my mother ... oh heck, I forgot you've already met her. Seems like a lifetime ago.'

Leisa waggled her head back and forth. 'Don't tell me you've forgotten that momentous occasion. Ha.'

'Oh you mean the charming Mike Crane who saved you from cardiac arrest?'

Leisa slapped his arm. 'No, dear little Brandon. How could you forget the little bloke who ruined your suit?'

'You remembered his name? I underestimated you. I'll have to keep an eye on you. You're trouble.'

'I thought I had graduated from that maligned category. I will hold this against you for the rest of time, Mike Randall.'

'I'd like to hold you against me,' Mike murmured.

'What did you say?'

'Nothing.'

'You do remember that you're a rubbish liar.'

The colonel shuffled into the kitchen to announce, 'that Myron fella is coming up the drive with a large woman and a group of people. What are we going to do?'

Myron had returned with his Ma, uncle and various relatives.

Mike heard the rumble of voices as Eleanor Mansfield's relatives walked around the house to the back door. One of them had rapped on the heavy front door, received no instant response.

Myron was a carbon copy of his rotund mother, who proved to be every bit as aggressive as her son. She threatened all manner of retributions in spite of Leisa reminding the woman of what the police had said.

'You're keeping secrets, missie. I can read it on yer face. You've still got money of hers. I'll bet my life on it.'

'I sent her clothes to the Salvation Army because you refused to collect her belongings, and now you come here accusing me. How would I have her money? You collected her bank books and purse from the police.'

The woman paled. She turned to an older man and slapped him. 'Arthur. You didn't tell me about that. You said you only had to go to the morgue to identify her.'

'Slipped me mind, pet,' said the man as the woman grabbed him by the ear. 'Where is it, ya useless mongrel?'

Mike stepped forward. 'There's nothing for you here. Miss Reid has done everything for you. You should be thanking her instead of this nonsense. Feel free to leave. Now.'

Leisa sighed as the group retreated down the driveway. 'Thank God they didn't bring the media.'

'There's not enough time to go to Shellharbour now,' Mike said. 'We'll go this evening. If that's okay with you, Leisa.'

Richard settled into a kitchen chair. 'Your father isn't a current client, Mike. I don't remember why I brought his file over to my office, but I was only employed to ensure that your mother received child support until you turned 21. Seems he was old fashioned that way. There's no mention of Eleanor Mansfield. No provision.' Richard shrugged. 'The payments started 24 years ago, so right after your father left I imagine. The payments were always paid from an international bank. From your father's regular wages. So I have no information on any other monies.'

'Thanks Richard,' said Mike. 'That's more than I hoped for. It tells me more than you know. In all my imaginings I never thought he would leave the country. I've thought of him as being with that Eleanor, having a batch of other kids with her.

She went to the media, broke the scandal. She was pregnant.'

'Hmm. You sure? We handled all his Australian payments. There were a few business ones in the beginning where he sold the business. He didn't get much for it. His creditors went for him with a vengeance, and his business was in as bad a state as his reputation. Everyone ditched him. His money wouldn't have lasted long overseas. And as I said, there's no mention of that woman, or any other child. Unless she went with him. I wouldn't know about that.'

Leisa gripped Mike's arm. 'She told me that she had never had a passport when I asked for identification for the room.'

'I can hand the files over to you officially if you see a solicitor, Mike. In the meantime, I'll contact his Cairo bank and see what else I can find out.' He stood and slipped the folder under his arm. 'Oh yes, and I would try and sort those intrusive relatives of the dead woman. You don't want to go through another media fracas.'

'Leisa. This is getting too complicated. Do you mind if I ring the solicitor my father used?' Mike asked.

'Of course not. None of the information you've learned is confidential to me. Go ahead.'

Mike shouldn't have been surprised when the call was answered swiftly. After all it was Gary Bradshaw's mobile number.

'Hello,' said a firm masculine voice. 'It's been a while. What can I do for you, young man?'

Mike outlined what they had found as Gary Bradshaw, KC, listened intently.

'You could go to the magistrate and get a restraining order, but I think from what you've told me of that family a simple letter should settle things. You don't owe then anything, although I do suggest you offer compensation on the wrecked bike. It it's worded correctly they should bother you again.'

'Wonderful. I appreciate that Gary … and about Dad?'

'Let me see what I can turn up, Mike.'

The visit with Mike's mother went well. Mike slipped outside to read the letter while Leisa sat with Marcia, Mike's mother.

They stopped at a café in Shellharbour. Hunger had kicked in after the stress of the day. It was a fast-food place with bright lights and cold hard chairs.

They ate hungrily when their food arrived.

'I noticed your mother's frailty, Mike.' Leisa attempted to tame her errant hair and relax her body.

'You're right,' said Mike. 'Mum has MS. You might have guessed there was something when you met her. Although she's very good at hiding it.'

Leisa nodded. She had noticed that his mother hadn't risen from the chair on her first visit, but had not spoken of it.

'Mum was diagnosed fifteen years ago, when I was a teen at school. She had a horrid time of it in the first few months. I covered for her, as she covered for me. We were so busy doing that for each other that we didn't ever seem to have time to talk about the past, or didn't want to.'

Surprise flitted across Leisa's face. 'You were her carer.'

Mike turned his head, opened his eyes. 'Oh, I don't know about that … I guess so. Look, I don't expect you to forgive me for concealing my identity.'

'… and lying,' Leisa finished, hiding a smile.

'Tsk, and lying,' said Mike, 'but living at the B&B the past few months has opened my eyes. I've been trying to persuade Mum to move in with me. What a fool I've been. Why would she want to…'

'…live in a city penthouse with a swinging bachelor?' Leisa chuckled.

'Oh ha ha, Miss Reid. There's no swinging … you think the worst of me don't you?'

Leisa shrugged.

'It's no wonder Mum has always said no to the idea. Stuck in an apartment building with no company, no view of the ocean.' Mike sighed.

'She's happy where she is, I think. I saw her love of the ocean.'

'I guess she'll never want to leave there.'

'Oh, I don't know. Nance might not be able to stay with her forever.'

'One eyebrow rose slightly as Mike twitched. 'You met Nance?'

'Yes, I helped her make scones. She'd just burned a batch. Probably because she was eavesdropping on my conversation with your mother, on your instructions. As you waited across the road in your Ute.'

'Is nothing sacred,' said Mike, smiling for the first time since he'd confessed the lie. 'I can't believe you noticed all that.'

Leisa leaned towards him. 'You didn't think much of me then, Mike Randall.'

'And now I think of you too much.' Mike chuckled and presented a hand to Leisa. 'Am I forgiven? Truly forgiven. Shall we shake on that?'

Leisa's hand was soft and warm. It also had some form of electric current. Mike wanted to both prolong the experience.

The dark interior of the car offered a more intimate setting. Leisa drew in a ragged breath as Mike adjusted her seat belt. Each of them was aware of the other in a new way.

'I guess we should get moving,' Mike said, reluctantly starting the car.

'I don't want to go home,' Leisa said quietly, staring at her hands.

'Would you like a slow country drive around the harbour? See the city lights?

Leisa laughed. 'You can't call it a country drive in the city,' Leisa said as she leaned the passenger seat back.

Mike laughed and turned the music down. 'We could stop here for a while.'

Leisa lowered the window and sniffed the salty air. 'This is marvellous. No wonder your mother loves living by the sea.'

The gulls had fled the kiosks and picnic areas leaving the ibises to poke their long beaks in the bins. Only a few lone walkers and entwined lovers dotted the sandy shores.

As the ocean breezes and the lapping of the waves stole their way into the Ute

Their murmured voices fill the void in the car as they exchanged more details of their lives.

They had no answers or conclusions, advice or judgement.

Mike told her of his phone conversation with the solicitor, and the solicitor's plans to look into Mike's father's whereabouts. 'He might get further than Richard. He was a real friend to Dad. I think he introduced Dad to Mum.'

Leisa was emboldened by Mike's revelations. 'My dad was much older than Mum. Twenty years. They made provisions for my future without a father, never suspecting that Mum would go first. Dad was devastated. The only way he could handle life was to escape everything familiar. But I had the opposite situation to you. Dad never stopped talking about Mum. Never looked at another woman. He didn't see them. Not even Marion, the woman he hired as a live-in housekeeper. Richard, his business partner ended up marrying her.'

'I can't imagine a love like that. A family like that.'

'Was it always an unhappy place, Mike? Your family?'

Mike put his hands over his face and sobbed violently.

Leisa reached for him, soothing and cooing.

'It was the happiest time of my life,' Mike said. He pulled the letter from his pocket. 'It's all here. In this letter. That woman had it for years. There was never a child, a pregnancy, but he didn't make excuses.'

Mike continued to sob. 'That's not the worst part.'

'Oh, Mike.' Leisa stroked his hair.

'She was only to give me the letter when he died. Oh Leisa, he's gone. He's gone.' Mike's shoulders convulsed. 'I never expected to feel this way. I've been to the darkest places in my mind and this was the last thing I thought would be the answer.

A father abroad earning a wage with demanding physical work. Punishing himself with hard labour. Dying there. A world away from home.'

Leisa snaked her arms around Mike and he pulled her to him, resting his cheek on her head.

'Do you want me to drive home,' asked Leisa.

'Thanks, but no. I'm going to be okay. I'm going to be okay now.'

Back at the house, laughter could be heard coming from the kitchen. The colonel was entertaining Cissy and Celia with the story of the Mansfield mob's latest visit.

'We went out for tea, Leisa. Don't worry about us. You look done in.' Celia rose from the table.

Cissy stared at Leisa and Mike, while those two realised that they had linked hands sometime in the past few hours and hadn't let go.

The colonel tilted his head in the direction of the loungeroom and the other boarders followed her lead, noisily scraping chairs.

'There's not much of summer left,' said Leisa, her voice rich with contentment.

'I love the change of seasons,' said Mike, alert to a change in her.

They were sitting at the small wrought iron table at the back of the limestone courtyard under the flame tree. The flame tree that was her secret connection with her departed mother. The tree was in that rare time of transition where both fruit and leaves resided; before the leaves fell one by one to embrace autumn.

A gentle evening breeze cart-wheeled the leaves around the table. A moonless twilight was gathering around them. It was so much more intimate tonight. The B & B guests had gone out to catch a dinner show, laughing gaily to Leisa, 'Don't wait up for us.' Leisa had been surprised when Mike arrived back at the guesthouse early.

He was so close she could smell sandalwood soap. His thick hair was damp, and she watched in fascination as water dripped from burnished copper curls that touched his T shirt. This was the first time she had seen him in casual T shirt and jeans. She had only ever seen him in his tradesmen work gear, or that first time, in a suit.

As he bent to casually caress Sal at his feet she allowed a moment to imagine his touch. Shaking free of the image she picked up a plate of cheese and biscuits. She needed to eat. The wine was going to her head. If she didn't stop that line of thought she would be fantasizing about other improbable things. Like how it would feel to wind her fingers through his lush damp hair. If she didn't look into those deep chocolate eyes she would be fine.

She regretted setting the smaller table now. One of the large picnic tables would have placed him at a reasonable distance.

Mike sensed her mellow mood. He'd been tense at work all afternoon without knowing why. He'd been staying away later to avoid her, and a growing attraction that surprised him. His earlier purpose to investigate her and her connection to his father's lover had evaporated. And yet he was still here. He nearly laughed out loud; he was turning out to be a very reluctant spy. He had wanted so much to see her as the conniving witch of his first imaginings, but at every turn she revealed another layer more attractive than the one before.

Leisa wondered at her new reaction to Mike. They had been physically closer before, laughing and handing tools and paint brushes as they tackled the upstairs rooms. Mike had even wandered in and out of her bedroom with its exotic Mid Eastern silks and tapestries. But it had been all business as he measured and gave her instructions to write down.

Something had shifted and she realised that it was trust. She trusted him. He had been protector. It was also his vulnerability to the trauma of his childhood. She admired the growth she had seen when he had faced the past and thrown bitterness aside, finding forgiveness.

It had been a long time since she had felt this relaxed with a man. She wasn't even sure if she had been alone with a man of her own age since her ex-boyfriend's violent argument. Mike had been at the B & B for two months and although she had noticed his dark eyes watching her, he hadn't made a move or even flirted.

He wanted her; she knew that, with the sure instincts of a woman. She put the wine glass down, needing a clear head.

This was a man who would never force or plead, making the pull towards him that much stronger.

He was silent now, watching her. Raising her eyes slowly to his she saw raw passion exposed in his dark eyes.

Leaning back in the chair casually, he held her gaze. The intensity took her breath away. His response to her was there for the reading. Not daring to tell him with words, she allowed her eyes to reveal her longing.

He reached out a hand to hers, drawing her slowly to him. She rose from her seat and moved towards him. With the exquisite ease of a ballroom dancer he drew her into his lap.

Caressing her face slowly and tenderly he left a tingling trail of response. He paused; then drew a gentle finger along the sweet curve of her bottom lip.

She moaned softly, cursing him for his patience. When she had tangled her willing fingers through the damp curls at the nape of his neck he bent his head towards her.

With soft deliberate control he possessed her mouth, beginning the tango of moist lips that ignited a rhythm in her surrendering heart. It was the lightest of kisses but her body was on fire.

Mum always said I acted before thinking. Oh crap! What had I done?

The man at my feet still had a pulse. Thank God for that! I felt sorry for a brief moment, then remembered the breaking of glass and the clunk of the lock when the front door had swung wide open several long minutes ago. Long enough for me to be out of bed, fully alert.

I had been sleep-deprived, I reasoned. Working 24 hour shifts in the Beauville Lodge for handicapped boys will do that to you. It wasn't my fault. We were often wakened to some crisis or other and sprang into action, 'feet to the floor', ready to protect our charges.

Why was I feeling bad for goodness' sake? I had just had a home invasion. The guy who ran through the door had brandished a crowbar, was wearing a balaclava and carrying a sack. It was just a shame I hadn't hit *him*, but had given the fellow that followed him a swift uppercut. My brother had shown me how. 'Smack your fist upwards into your attacker's jaw as if you're aiming for the ceiling, Emma. They'll be out like a light,' he said.

It had worked like a treat. The man at my feet was testament to that. However, I was experiencing strong doubts that my victim had anything to do with the lowlife who'd broken in and taken off like greased lighting when I screamed.

For one thing the man on the floor was barefoot, and I was pretty sure no self-respecting burglar would go on a crime spree minus footwear.

My suspicions of his innocence were increased by the fact that he was bare-chested. It was also worrying that his thick head of mahogany hair was unruly, as if, like me, he had been wakened suddenly. He was wearing grey track pants and hadn't been carrying anything that I could see.

I quickly dialled 000, then wondered whether to say ambulance or police. I chose ambulance.

There was a soft murmur from the man. I approached him tentatively and knelt by his head again. He must be regaining consciousness. His pulse was regular. I looked at his broad chest. His breathing was steady. At least he hadn't hit the tile floor too hard. He'd slumped against the wrought iron baker's stand on the way down.

I would never forget the look of shocked surprise on his face; he'd probably never been hit by a woman. Come to think of it, I'd never hit a man. I was beginning to wish I hadn't hit this one. His masculine face was tanned by the sun, but there was nothing to hint at a criminal career.

In his unconscious state he looked a little vulnerable, even with a 5 o'clock shadow. There were no ominous tattoos or piercings. In fact, he wouldn't have looked out of place in an advertisement for men's cologne.

Damn, where was that ambulance? There was still no

movement from the man. Then the front room was flooded with light from the ambulance headlights. Thank God, they were here. They wasted no time assessing the man; I gave them a brief, slightly sanitised version of the home invasion.

'I didn't phone the police, though,' I muttered, feeling uncomfortable.

'So this guy broke into your house?' inquired a slim efficient ambulance officer, his pen poised.

'Well, not exactly,' I murmured. 'There was another guy who broke the lock and came in, then this man here came rushing in after him.'

The ambulance man flashed me a confused look. I squirmed.

'So you think they were working together?'

I shrugged, feeling less sure of myself by the second.

'Never mind, love, the police will sort it out. They'll be here in a jiffy.' A frisson of panic gripped me. I had visions of being hauled off in handcuffs. He flashed me a reassuring smile. I was not reassured. 'You work at that group home for teens don't you? Haven't we seen you there? We ambos get called out there a bit.'

His companion nodded.

'Yes, I do six 24 hour shifts a fortnight,' I said, relieved. At least they knew me, and were not looking at me as if I was a violent maniac.

'So, you don't know this guy at all?'

'Nope. I've lived here for years, and I don't think I've ever seen him,' I said. Then a memory stirred of a removal van in the street a few doors up on the other side. 'Oh dear,' I added, suddenly feeling sick to my stomach.

The ambos lightly bandaged his head, taking care with his jaw that was fast swelling and where dark bruising was appearing. They applied a neck brace, then transferred him deftly onto the trolley using a spinal board.

'Well, we're ready to take him to Southwest General.'

'I'm coming with you.'

So just like that, I walked out the door in my hot pink pyjamas, grabbing my mobile phone as I went and my new snakeskin handbag. As I said, Mum always said I acted before I thought.

As they pushed the trolley up into the ambulance, the man fluttered charcoal eyelashes, opening his eyes briefly to reveal deep chocolate eyes that registered pure terror when he saw me, before passing out again.

'He was conscious for a second,' I informed the ambo who was driving, as I settled into the front seat. I didn't mention my casual observation that Mr Unconscious was heart-stoppingly handsome. That was hardly a relevant medical detail. Only *my* pulse was affected by that knowledge.

By the time they had begun assessing the mystery man in the Accident & Emergency Ward, I had woken my best friend, Victoria.

'Oh, for God's sake, Emma, it's 3 am! What have you done this time?' shrieked Victoria.

'I can't help it if trouble finds me. I've had an attempted burglary. They must have thought the house was empty. My car was at the mechanics being serviced. Never mind the whole story. Just tell me what you know about the new people who moved into the house opposite. It's an emergency.'

'It wasn't one of our properties, but I'll get hold of Lance from Banker Realty and get back to you.' Victoria was a real estate agent, as well as a miracle worker.

The attending Accident & Emergency doctor was Dr Jean Blake. I knew her well. She was a passionate fundraiser for the Home. We'd also met many times when I escorted teens for assessments, or stayed with them during hospital visits.

By the time Doctor Jean returned, I had the mystery man's name and a few sketchy details. He was Jake Melville, the CEO of *Computer Solutions*, and I had broken his jaw in two places. What I hadn't been able to find out was anything about his family. Victoria's friend Lance knew nothing about any possible next of kin.

'Well, Emma, they have to operate now,' Jean said, looking over her glasses and tapping her clipboard.

Two theatre attendants arrived with a trolley.

I burst into tears.

'It's all my fault,' I bawled miserably.

'Don't feel too bad. It's a mistake anyone could make.'

'Thanks for letting me stay with him, Jean.'

'Well you've been the only one able to find out his identity. And anyway...' her eye twinkled, 'you're hardly a threat to society. You've got enough credibility here. Mind you, you'll never live down the "right hook" jokes from the staff. Oh...' She turned to leave. '...*and the hot pink PJ's!*'

'Crap, I forgot.'

Jake likes to play Scrabble and is astonishingly good at it for a computer geek. He hates it when I call him that, but I've discovered that a man with a wired jaw has a greatly compromised ability to argue.

Yes, we're on a first name basis now.

The newspaper lapped up the story and I've become used to being the butt of jokes. 'Vigilante Homeowner Hits Wrong Guy', 'Crazed Martial Arts Homeowner Packs a Punch', 'Good Samaritan Out Cold', and my personal favourite 'CEO of Computer Solutions Hospitalised over Home Invasion Gone Wrong'. I liked this one as it almost made Jake sound as though he was in the wrong. Which, technically, he was—sort of anyway. I was most put out by being accused of having martial arts experience. I only went to a meeting once. I couldn't even twist myself into the starting position, and was told my 'war cry' wouldn't scare a mouse.

For a man who can't talk, Jake can certainly get his point across. Scribbles instructions like a Major General. Must drive his secretary nuts. Come to think of it, he did— drive her nuts, that is. She came to sit and take notes, but couldn't stand the ward and its smells because she's in the first trimester of pregnancy. So she left. Which is how I ended up doing his letters, making his business phone calls and rearranging his diary. Naturally.

Well, I was there anyway. Driven by deep compassion to help, and *not* by guilt, as Jake uncharitably claims. I was already feeding and shaving him, so what was a bit of extra work? The nurses were grateful as they were terminally busy. I didn't mind helping out. When Jake was offered a bed at a ritzy private hospital with around-the-clock nurses to special him—the pigheaded man refused to go. I think he did it to punish me.

He addresses me as Ms New Sance, at the top of his notes to me.

'Ha ha, funny man,' I said. 'I'll give *you* nuisance.'

YOU ALREADY DID, he scribbled.

'I don't think capital letters are necessary. No wonder your secretary left,' I accused, muttering 'pompous prat' under my breath.

I HEARD THAT!

'If you keep using capital letters to intimidate me, I'm leaving too,' I threatened.

I'VE NEVER BEEN ASSAULTED, AND THEN INSULTED BY THE SAME WOMAN, scribbled His Royal Pain in the Arse.

'Oh, you usually keep those two separate, do you Sweet Cheeks? Clever you!'

I'VE SACKED PEOPLE FOR LESS THAN THIS.

'Really, so there's just you and Ms Morning Sickness left in the company then?' He got a triple word score then—on my word! 'You can't sack someone you don't pay, you cheapskate,' I retorted.

No-one pays someone who regularly threatens the boss.

'Well, good for you, you're beginning to learn not to use capitals. There might be hope for you yet, you ungrateful man. Now, about my wages. How about I threaten you *irregularly?*'

You always have an answer for everything? He wrote.

Just then he reached out to grab my hand to stop me sneaking one of his scrabble tiles. I would have answered, but my fingers were having a strange reaction – neurologically speaking, of course, but the tingling stopped my brain, and inevitably my mouth. He grinned.

Bother, he knew he was affecting me and enjoying it, I thought. If I blushed, I'd have to pretend to pick something off the floor. If only he'd let my hand go I'd be able to think.

This "helping him out deal" was getting complicated. I began to wonder why I was there, my motives were getting fuzzy. My hand was still buzzing after I left.

I might need a doctor myself. I told myself not to be daft; I was only there for completely innocent charitable reasons. But just in case, I cleaned the whole house so I wouldn't think about him, I mean the buzzing thing.

It was just lucky for him that my supervisor at the group home forced me to take stress leave, or I wouldn't have become so bored that I decided to take care of him at all. Just to make things clear I told him the next day he should pay me. That should get things back in the right direction.

You're on stress leave, you can't get paid twice! he scribbled.

'You should be nicer to someone on stress leave.'

They put you on stress leave because YOU WERE STRESSING THEM! He wrote furiously.

'Arrggh! *Again with the capitals!* It's the equivalent of yelling, you know. This is workplace harassment. And I was *not* "stressing them". They just got sick of the television camera crews in the front yard of the Home. Let's not lose sight of who's the victim here.'

Jake just rolled his eyes (did I mention gorgeous chocolate brown) and threw down the pen, after writing, *I give up.*

'I win?' I crowed with glee, picking up the Scrabble tiles.

NO!!!!! My score is double yours!

'Exclamation marks now—I should call a lawyer. Did I tell you I hate Scrabble?'

Only a thousand times already!

We were interrupted by Jake's specialist, who was a gentle Pakistani and also the surgeon who operated on him.

'Mr Melville, you are ok to go home. This pleases you, yes?'

Jake's beaming grin said it all.

'Your wife … she is taking good care of you, no?' asked Dr Nahoo, smiling shyly at me.

'I'm not...' I began, but Jake's hand snaked out and trapped mine, stopping me mid-sentence. I looked down at our hands intertwined. I think I blushed, but I wouldn't admit that, not even under torture.

We're getting married as soon as I recover. Jake wrote. Dr Nahoo read the note aloud. He was all gleaming smiles and congratulations. Enthusiastically shaking our hands, he called the staff in. They became excited, saying how wonderful it was. Fate, they'd seen it coming. I hadn't, or had I?

'So, Jake Melville, does this mean I'm relegated to playing Scrabble for the rest of my life?' I asked, after the staff left.

Unless you can think of more interesting games.

'Anyone could think of more interesting things to do than Scrabble,' I said, as he pulled me towards him.

I wondered briefly how a man could melt you with a kiss when his jaw was wired.

They didn't find the burglar, which is just as well. It would be highly inappropriate to thank someone who had intended to rob you blind.

One day lost

If I began at the beginning, where would I begin? It became the love story of Emily and Angelo, but I did not know it then, and neither did they.

It began in childhood, or more correctly, on the brink where the edges of childhood are blurring into that deliciously confusing world of adulthood. But, this story doesn't belong in childhood. The story where their lives began to weave together began when Emily was 14 and Angelo was 16, and it still goes on and will go on forever, still intertwined and increasing in love.

Angelo was the new boy at school. But he had confidence that no new boy ever had before, or after him. Even though he had a decidedly dorky name, no one cared. He was gorgeous. Lithe and slim with the bearing of a dancer, he had all the air of a Latin lover at just 16. And the girls sighed and wept in equal portions.

At sixteen, he was enchanted by the female sex but wary. There was a world-weary essence about him as he rolled his eyes, as if he'd seen it all before. Perhaps he had, for he was one of seven—the other six being girls. His family was Spanish, his parents stereotypically Mediterranean. The daughters laughed and said they were straight off TV.

A single sentence never contained only one language in their home. Mario and Brigitte would roll effortlessly between the two languages without seeming to know they had crossed over. The girls were a mixture of the two worlds, but Angelo was pure Aussie male. Girls were sheilas and any Latin sensitivities he would possess, he developed later, if ever.

Angelo had never lived in Spain, spoke no Spanish and didn't give a toss about anything Spanish. He didn't play down his heritage to fit in - he was just indifferent, living in the moment. Because he didn't see the difference, he was generally affronted when approached by some breathless teenage girl who wanted him to say something in Spanish, or better still sing something (he was reputed to be 'into' music.

These overtures were met with bewilderment and a fairly terse and disappointingly Aussie response, 'Get real, I don't know any frigging Spanish.'

Any expectation that this would discourage the female species was squashed by their giggles of adoration. With black hair curling onto his forehead, generous lips, and smoky eyes, they didn't care what he said. It was when his aloofness became swaggering arrogance that Emily and Angelo became close, or at least aware of each other. It could hardly be said that they became friends, because the sparks of awareness made that possibility difficult.

Emily was far more shocked than he by the strength of their attraction. A combination of total ignorance of all things sexually related, and a romantic nature, made for a lethal cocktail on Emily's part. As for Angelo, he was playing his cards so close to his chest that Emily wondered if even he knew what they were. She only knew that she moved him and he moved her more than any other boy had. And with the passion of the very young she just knew that no one else ever would or could.

It was both a beautiful and painful awakening. For such passion so early and so young had nowhere to go but sadness and confusion. They were both so uneasy it would be a year of smouldering glances before they would again risk an encounter after a muggy spring day when they shared their first kiss. And embrace.

Even though it was the most innocent of soft embraces it shook Emily to the core with the unexpected yearning it produced. The aching tenderness of it blindsided her. Coming from a home where her father was austere and remote, and her mother dominating and cheerless, she was totally unprepared for the wave of new emotions.

Other boys had carried her school bag home, but she waved them goodbye with a cheery salute. Suddenly she was being held in the arms of someone male and strong, and she didn't want to ever move away from him.

***

'*It had been a day of endless magic*'…bother…that was too flowery. Emily chewed the end of her pen and lay back on the porch swing that held pride of place in the small courtyard at the back of her grandparents' house. Resting her hand on her swollen belly she groaned at the task before her.

It had seemed like such a simple idea when she sat in the counsellor's rooms trying to make some sense of the dilemma

72

her life had become. The more pregnant she became, the less it seemed to matter that she try and recall the events that caused the miracle inside her.

Today, like so many other times, she struggled to remember the day she had lost. Not just any day, mind you, but the day she'd lost her virginity and conceived the child she was carrying. She was just so tired of trying to see this memory as so all-important when she felt such joy at the life within her. This precious miracle that was somehow uniquely hers and hers alone.

She went quite willingly to the counsellor because she had no fear, no painful longing, just a nagging gap in her mind. She realised her mother, Ethel's insistence she attend counselling was prompted by the conviction that Emily would 'see sense' and abort her unborn child. Her mother's goodwill fled when she realised Emily had no intention to terminate the pregnancy.

All the usual tools of parental blackmail were used by her mother. Strident recriminations followed by tearful begging. Loud and blustering demands to 'think of us'. Exhortation for Emily to see reason and not ruin her life (and theirs by proxy).

'Pray about it dear,' her mother said. 'Pray hard.'

Emily had, as she knelt on the hard wooden floor of the little timber church.

'Just one day, one tiny day, is that too much to ask, God?' No revelation was forthcoming. Didn't God owe her a day?

***

And now, sitting in the canvas swing that had held her childhood secrets, Emily sighed. Not for lost innocence and a marred future, but with the sheer relief that she was in a place of serenity. A place where it didn't matter a jot what the world outside thought or did. There was no world outside the high-walled rose garden of her grandparents' home.

She smiled softly at Nana Jessie's huge, tabby cat as he eyed the goldfish in the outdoor pond malevolently, if somewhat impotently. 'You're too well fed, Jasper, you're not fooling anyone with that hunting routine.'

He gazed back, and as if in agreement he jumped up on the swing and curled around her feet purring majestically.

'I'm not fooling anyone either, Jasper,' she sighed as the stroked his thick, soft fur. 'Doing assignments for school was easier than this.'

Emily put down the pen, laid her head on the tasselled pillow, then followed Jasper's example and stretched. The known to the unknown was the idea. Writing down any thoughts or memories no matter how sketchy or tentative was supposed to recreate that day in her head. A memorable day that her mind refused to remember. How ironic. She had tried desperately to remember and piece the day together. Tried and failed.

It was because of the accident that she'd lost her memory, in the first place. The doctors said it was not uncommon for people to lose a few days, weeks or even years after an accident. As accidents go, it hadn't been terribly traumatic physically. Just a mild concussion. And the other events of the day had assumed epic proportions compared to what seemed like a little slip of the mind at the time.

She had been riding pillion on the back of her brother's bike, when he slewed around the corner, throwing her off the bike. Paul had stepped away from the bike unharmed. He'd been wearing a helmet, whereas Emily hadn't. Not many riders, much less their pillion passengers bothered in small country towns in the Sixties. Her brother's arrest had made her memory loss seem insignificant. That is, until her mother had taken her to the doctor for gastro, where they received the shocking revelation that Emily was 12 weeks pregnant.

Ethel was one of those women who built their egos on the skeletons left over from the gossip mill. And for the first time in her life, she was at the epicentre of not one, but two scandals. In her worst nightmares she could not have imagined such chaos. She could not fathom why Paul had been arrested for 'speeding and negligent driving causing grievous bodily harm'. She seemed to have forgotten the many police warnings that had been directed at her son for his hooligan antics. She appeared to have no concept of Paul meeting his consequences. He'd only been letting off steam on those previous occasions with no harm done.

Of course, if she had been at the local police station she would have heard the rancour from the officers about finally 'nailing that hoon and throwing the book at him'. With many of them being fathers, the thought of Paul speeding was bad enough, but to be wearing a helmet and leave his sister without one was frankly unforgiveable.

***

Emily massaged her swollen belly and pondered her dilemma. It seemed to cause the whole wide world more stress and anxiety than it did her. To everyone else it was crucial she remember that lost day.

Were pregnancy hormones affecting her mind? The more time passed, the less important it seemed to remember the day that had been so completely erased from her mind, by an accident she had no control over. Maybe she was just tired of prodding a reluctant brain.

Right then, she decided it didn't matter- not how or who or why. This child was. And this child was hers.

And would always be hers if she found the courage to claim this miracle, this baby. She would no longer spend time trying to solve the mystery. In that moment of ownership, she discovered a different truth than she had been adjured to seek.

This child was not profane; it was sacred. Her baby was not a mistake. This child was part of her, of who she was, and the woman she was to become.

She cast aside the dreadful scenes with her mother, when she had been accused of everything from drunkenness to insanity. She knew she had not been drunk then or ever, no accident would wipe her basic soul away. How dare they accuse her of being anything other than what she had always been?

And even though she retained no shred of memory, she knew in her heart that she had not been raped or abused. She had no explanations to give to her family and she would give them none, even though her mother tirelessly reminded her that she owed them that at least.

She couldn't owe them what she didn't have. She would give

them the truth, nothing more. Nothing less. She tore the page into satisfying little strips and began to write quickly and concisely all of the plans and the people she would need in her life with her child and their future.

The first step would be to tell her grandparents of her decision - and then her parents.

Emily had no illusions that she could depend on bringing this child into her parent's home. Thank God for Nana and Grandy.

The pen fell from her hand as she remembered Grandy's shining eyes when she walked through their door.

'She'll be okay,' he said, arms outstretched.

There had been a wealth of understanding in his eyes. And something more—trust. He trusted her - her actions as well as her decisions, and he would move heaven and earth to stand by her side.

Telling her grandparents she had chosen to keep her baby had been relatively easy compared to the nuclear fallout of telling her parents, or more precisely the fallout of telling her mother, Ethel. It was then Emily realised just how large a stake her mother had invested in Emily giving her baby up for adoption. She wasn't sure which was worse, the tears or the anger, the proclamations of love or the accusations, as Ethel swerved mercilessly between the two.

When Ethel delivered the ultimatum that it was abortion or adoption, it had never occurred to her that her studious, submissive daughter would do anything other than comply with one or the other.

It was inconceivable that she, Ethel, would have to face the shame of not only a pregnant daughter, but one who lived with her paternal grandparents. Thank God Leonard's parents lived three hours away. She'd be able to invent reasons for Emily's absence until she came to her senses. As she surely would.

Aiming at a show of solidarity Ethel had insisted the whole family visit to sort out the problem. Even Paul, who normally found a way around his mother, had been beaten into submission by the sheer weight of her determination.

Ethel was running out of patience.

They had been discussing things for four hours she had and gained no leeway. She hadn't come to sit here on the patio of her husband's parents, politely pretending to enjoy afternoon tea, to be thwarted at every turn.

'Of course I don't my only daughter on the street with no roof over her head and no food in her stomach,' she said.

The superior attitude that accompanied this protestation suggested otherwise.

'I am ready to welcome my daughter back to my care and the hearth of home,' Ethel added.

This speech faltered a little when Paul said they hadn't a hearth because they were peasants.

'I got myself into this mess; I'll find a way out - without giving up my child,' said Emily.

This calm statement only served to provoke Ethel.

'A great many more people will be required to get you out of this mess, than the one who got you into it. A great number of people who didn't choose this particular mess, and who have offered solutions that haven't been listened to, much less heeded.' Ethel drew breath.

Emily chose that moment to retort, 'A great number of people called Ethel?'

'You can all go to hell!' yelled Ethel.

It was a moment of fine hysteria, and what the statement lacked in theological standing, it made up for in its ability to end the painful interchange.

Everyone knew that when Ethel consigned anyone to hell, it was over. Turning her back on Emily and her in-laws, Ethel grabbed her handbag.

Then, Paul, who had just been released from his two month sentence in the local jail, was offered the privilege of driving Ethel and Leonard home.

'Paul, dear, you've paid your debt to society. You need to get back in the saddle and hold your head high,' said Ethel, if only to emphasise the point that she was no longer talking to the others.

Paul found this casting of him in the light of Restored and Reformed much to his liking, and took leave of everyone with a newly superior nod of the head.

Nobody corrected Ethel's parting statement, but there was little surprise in that, nobody ever corrected Ethel. She barrelled forward with the certain conviction beating in her large bosom that saying her piece would bring everyone around. It was only a matter of time before the family would be restored to its original form and everyone would admit she had been right, and wonder why they hadn't listened sooner.

Ethel ran this scenario around her head a few times and liked it more and more. The others thought it strange to see a small triumphant smile play on her lips as Paul careened out the driveway, throwing gravel and nearly unseating Leonard, who'd been relegated to the back seat.

Emily and her grandparents went back into house where they sank wordlessly into the comforting depths of the faded lounge with the cabbage roses. Grandy in the recliner, Nana Jessie in the rocker, and Emily in the love seat, her feet up.

How simply and effortlessly they each found their favourite place, Emily thought, as she looked at the beloved and worn faces of the two people who had 'gone to bat' for her. How different was this place, this home? It was as if the seats were just like the soul of the house—a special place for everyone where you were a perfect fit.

Her murky future seemed clearer and brighter. This was reality, this was home. She could close her eyes and see a tiny, bright new person running with arms outstretched.

Her dreams were not over, they were just beginning. She hadn't destroyed her life simply by creating another, and she would move heaven and earth to make sure her child, this child of grace, would never feel it was a mistake.

Grace, that was a lovely name—maybe if she had a girl she would call her Grace.

***

Grandy looked around the room at his two favourite women and smiled at the likeness between them. Feisty and feminine. Cool-headed with logic, and warmth combined with love. Women of grace.

It seemed strange (no, not strange - just new) to think of Emily as a woman, but she was. For all the fuss and bother about a child having a child, Emily would be 18 in a week, and he had no doubt that she was more than capable of raising this child.

Why if that bossy, sour-mouthed Ethel could raise a gem like Emily, anyone could see that even on her own Emily had more than a fighting chance. He wasn't a gambling man, but he'd lay odds on Emily doing it, and doing it well. And she would add that special way she had of savouring every moment and 'extracting the best'.

A chuckle escaped from deep down in his chest at the thought of Ethel having to bow to the one person who'd ever defied her—her daughter.

He might be wicked, but he had enjoyed that day of reckoning. He wasn't going to miss this adventure for the world, and he thanked the gods for the good fortune that had landed his incredible granddaughter in his lap for another few rounds with life.

***

Nana Jessie leaned back in the faded rocker and finally allowed herself to take a long slow breath. She had watched her husband of over four decades knot and unknot his rheumatic hands. She relaxed as soon as he rested them on the arms of the recliner. As she watched the slight ripples of sleep twitch across his brown, lined face she marvelled again at her good fortune in life. She would choose this moment in life to be happy.

As she gently rocked and watched the other two she smiled a slow, indulgent smile. Let Ethel with her unerring compass for the negative, cover the dark side of the situation - heaven only knew she was up for the task. But Jessie would not travel down that road.

Contrary to what Ethel said, Jessie knew exactly what she was getting herself into by taking in this warm and witty girl, who already loved and adored her – a love that was returned. This was her chance too, and she would make sure it was Emily's.

Today had been a proud day for Jessie—to see Emily claim her place in the world as a woman. She had bristled in anger at the inference that Emily would 'fail and come crawling home'.

Emily had already shown maturity beyond her years. While many of her peers were chasing boys and partying, Emily was often wrapped up in her room with a book. This 'child' knew how to be a woman.

Everyone talked about how much Emily had to offer the world and how those hopes were blighted.

Ethel had made much of the notion that Emily's childhood was over, but Jessie mourned that Emily's childhood had been over before it began. She remembered a little girl sitting alone. A little girl with a joyous smile that would light up anyone's world, and a giggle as outrageous as it was spontaneous.

***

Emma stood alone at Angelo's memorial, tiny, shining tears slipped silently down each cheek. Tears that were unbidden and unchecked. More genuine than any of the surrounding finery that celebrated the passing of a life. The perfect scrolls of printed words on parchment. The perfect wreaths, vibrant with life and discordant with the soil they rested on.

Emily clutched her bouquet of wildflowers and dandelions that she'd brought as a tribute to the love she barely knew—the man she had adored, and better still admired.

There was a world of difference between her simple flowers and the divine display before her. This same distance had existed in her relationship to the man she now mourned as poignantly as anyone ever mourned a lost love. A distance marked by mismatched timing, separation, and the misunderstood gestures of love's first awakening.

She remembered love's first kiss. A tender mingling to speak of hope and promise. The kiss she experienced was full of tremulous anticipation and breathless delight. Angelo had added desire—damn him. She was angry with him for crystallising desire and bringing the painful emotion of yearning.

And how she loved him. In that poignant moment she'd known heaven and hell. She had been introduced to the most difficult emotion she would ever deal with—Hope. One joyous moment away from heartbreak or happiness. She had not known which then, but she knew now.

Wise beyond her years, she had known that she had come close to something wonderful. And this she could take away with her today. This she could claim. This gift of admiration, this respect.

For just a small parcel of time she had bathed in the sunlight of his awe of her. For a moment she had danced with the gods, she had walked with angels. She had that memory, that small piece of him, the best man she'd ever known.

She smiled softly as she dropped the last of the flowers on

the new earth of Angelo's grave. They were only petals now, having been twisted and torn in her hands. The wrenching of her hands had been the only outward sign of her grief.

Her calm warmth and gentle touch to the other mourners belied the emotions that swam wildly in her heart. Had she been playing a part to feign composure on such a day as this? No, the world would not give her permission to mourn this man, this love because he had never belonged to her.

It hadn't been difficult to follow his career as he rose to fame as a celebrated cellist. Although he rarely graced the society pages, he had been referred to as a personable man, if somewhat solitary. They had crossed paths on occasion. Emily had been shocked to relive the same feelings, their power undiminished, his eyes still seeking.

And now, with everyone gone, she gave herself permission to mourn the man who had never known he was loved by her.

As she turned away from the grave, she glanced briefly up into the clear blue sky and wondered if he looked down on her now and understood. Was there anyone there with him? In her imagination she saw him turn to a faceless, cosmic companion and say, in his quiet soft, way—'She loved me best of all didn't she.'

She adjusted the snappy little black hat that added simple elegance to the basic black dress she wore. It shaded her from the relentless sun and the prying eyes of others. She wouldn't wear the dress again and she'd surprised herself by wearing it at all. In fact, she had never worn all black to a funeral before. In a kind of rebellious gesture to the bleakness of death she always wore something dark, with a splash of colour in defiance of that final sentence.

But today she'd added no touch of colour. There was no defiance today, for death had won, utterly and completely. Not only was Angelo gone, but he would never know her love.

Angelo. She repeated his name soft and low into the gentle breeze that was beginning to pick up the fallen leaves and swirl them up from this earth and take them to another place.

Angelo, where are you going? Are you an angel now? Are you the memory I lost? I can't imagine anyone else being Grace's father. But why can't I remember?

***

And this is where he found her. Among the weeping willows with their delicate narrow leaves trailing gently in the creek. In the frivolous flower-strewn dress Grace had chosen for her that morning resplendent with promise.

There had been a quality about that day since waking at dawn. The creek was moving as if it too knew of change and promise. The recent rains had made the old creek hurry and worry the eroding banks. The cement weir under the bridge once again had a fine misty waterfall flowing into the once muddy surge.

Grace had fretted over her this morning, child becoming mother, daughter gentling the nurturer—completing the cycle of love and life. Emily had resisted half-heartedly and then acquiesced to her determined daughter. She wore the dress.

At first she thought she was dreaming.

He was just the way she last remembered him. Unruly curls falling into his cloudy sensuous eyes. Lithe body stretched casually into faded, torn blue denims. He was resting against the old paper bark tree with both hands in his pockets.

'This creek is disgusting, muddy horrible thing,' she said.

The words shot out unbidden and unrehearsed. She bit her tongue. What would he think of her? But he was laughing, a full throated joyous sound.

'That's what you said on that day too.'

'What day?'

'The day God owes you.'

Emily sucked in her breath too quickly for a response.

'Yes, Emma, I am here to give you back that day.' He came and sat down beside her, cross-legged. A hidden memory sparked. He splayed his large hands on the checked blanket as if to show her some smooth secret blueprint.

She dared not breathe as his brown eyes captured her's. He held her heart in the palm of his hand. 'It was here wasn't it?'

He nodded.

'I should have known.'

'You have always known.'

His gentle eyes bid her silent, and she obeyed. He reached out one strong brown arm and encircled her, swinging her around to rest against his chest. A kookaburra laughed. The creek sang. A cricket burred. Emily melted into yesterday.

***

She was seventeen. In the frothy party dress she felt out of place at the creek. Throwing her strappy sandals on the ground she swore. She was too angry to cry. Why had her mother insisted she go with her brother to the party with his friends? It was bad enough having to tolerate their leers and winks at home.

Emily had dawdled and fiddled, hoping he would leave without her, but he'd called out, 'Come on sis, hurry up.'

The party had been a disaster, or the beginning had. She hadn't stayed for long. The party went on without her. After being trapped twice against the kitchen fridge by Paul's mate, Keith, with the wandering hands, who was making a precarious start on the banned alcohol, she bolted.

She would have to return. As much as she wanted to phone her parents to come and get her, she didn't want to get her brother into trouble. It was bad enough that she would have to go home on the back of his motorbike, trying to avoid burning her leg on the exhaust, while holding her floating white dress.

They would both be in trouble for that. Their parents thought the bike was safely in the shed, and that they were being driven home.

Cross and hot, she climbed down the embankment to the fort in the eucalypts where she intended to hide until the party was over. She could still hear the raucous male voices intermingled with girlish giggles floating through the cool afternoon air.

And there she found Angelo swimming in the creek with his dark curls plastered down his smiling brown face.

'This creek is a disgusting, muddy horrible thing.'

'You cannot say that from your high horse, river nymph,' He was laughing at her.

She laughed.

'You didn't mind it the last time we were here.'

She blushed. He remembered. It had been where they'd

shared their first kiss.

'So, if I'm a river nymph, are you Neptune, ruler of the deep?'

'Why don't you come in here and find out.'

And it was a simple as that. Two young hearts leaving childhood, unready for the world, but prepared for love. She stripped to her bra and pants and bombed him with an outrageous shriek.

'And what brings you here, fair maiden?'

'I have escaped a fire-breathing boy with arms like an octopus.'

Angelo was immediately still in the water and leashed his arm around her like an avenging archangel.

'What happened? Tell me.'

With a defiant tilt of her chin Emily began to form the words, but was stopped by his sweet hot mouth on hers. With the kiss of the cool water to guide them, their passion ignited slowly and tenderly.

'I have waited to do this a very long time,' he breathed against her slick, smooth forehead. 'But you ignored me. I watched you.'

'You withdrew from me.' She was plaintive now.

'We were children warming ourselves by the heat of an adult fire.'

They became playful. They were still. He told her of his latest composition, and talked of the master cellist he would study under for a year in Spain. He would be gone in a few weeks. She spoke of fashion design, clothing made from silken threads and nubbly wools. Her art spun into dreams, her dreams into art. They spoke of everything; except his leaving.

He showed her the hidden place under the burgeoning waterfall and found the secret places of her body and soul. They sat side by side under the waterfall in a world of their own, holding hands. With cement at their cool young backs they were cocooned with only the roaring sheet of the water in front of them.

No sounds entered their world that they did not choose or invite.

No words were said. No promises made.

They made love later, when breathless and chilled, they lay in the tree house.

'Angelo.'

'Emily.'

Twilight turned to night. She slept. Under the watchful eyes of her first lover. In his arms.

And when she left, he leant against the paper bark with his hands in the pockets of his torn blue jeans, his eyes a secret. She stopped at the edge of the clearing, turned and said, 'You never said goodbye.'

'You never said hello.'

***

'Angelo.'

Her heart was light as a cloud. Like a cloud shredded and scattered over the sky. How could she experience fullness and emptiness at the same time? All the questions she ever wanted to ask, he answered, with his seeking brown eyes, as he held both her hands in his.

She closed her eyes and leant back into his arms once more. She wrapped her own slim pale arms around his strong brown ones and clasped both their hands together in front of her, their fingers intertwined. Everything was still. She felt lightness. Her breath and all the air around swept upward, drawn to another place.

She thought him gone.

The only sound she heard was the scuttling of the leaves as they spiralled upwards, whirling rhythmically around the paperbark trees. She opened her eyes to bring back something familiar to her scattered mind. She looked for her old friend the creek.

She saw it all, yet far, far below, a woman asleep against the paperbark with that quiet smile Angelo said she wore. She saw herself, with the gentle breeze now stirring her long wild hair, as it fell over their entwined hands. She could still feel his arms around her as they were lifted high among the whispering clouds.

'You never said goodbye,' she whispered to the wind, in sweet remembrance of that time long gone.

'I came to say hello.'

Letters to a Soldier

To be fair, Laura Holden hadn't intended to start trouble. In truth, she'd been trying to avoid it. Or that is what she told herself at the beginning.

It would have been too great a ruse to claim that she had been trying to protect her sister Evangeline because everyone knew there was little love lost between the sisters on occasion. However, Laura had been truly happy for Evangeline at the engagement party organized by their parents at Heron Ave, in Vaucluse, Sydney.

The handsome soldier with his understated British appeal had charmed everyone in the family and especially Laura, who hoped for a fairytale love like her sister.

Laura stepped into her sister's affairs with tender-hearted concern and started a chain of events that would cross continents and wars. All to protect her sister's fiancé, Lance Corporal Roger Brown of Cheltenham, London, England, soon to be deployed to the theatre of the Second World war on foreign soil, God knows where.

It had started with a hardboiled egg and a demand. Laura was not one to take kindly to demands, especially after she had performed an act of generosity – on this occasion making her sister a hardboiled egg for breakfast.

Evangeline's tirade that she preferred soft boiled eggs had stirred latent anger in Laura. Coming right after the decision to be more caring and understanding of her sister had been the proverbial last straw. Well, perhaps the second last straw, because after that, when Evangeline switched to a simpering request that Laura deliver a letter to Private Roger Brown at the train station, Laura saw red. As the words to deny the request formed on her lips, she bit her tongue instead.

Her insatiable curiosity had been aroused. Why was Evangeline not farewelling her erstwhile suitor at the station herself? It wasn't as if there was a family crisis preventing her from keeping the appointment. And their accommodating parents had welcomed the news of Evangeline and Roger's engagement with casual indifference, and no sign of protest about the brevity of their acquaintance.

Forcing a smile on her face, and stuffing the sealed envelope into her handbag, Laura escaped to the park, where on a seat hidden in the shrubs, she had broken every rule of sisterhood, torn open the letter and read it.

The contents aroused such fury that she wandered along Darcy Street for hours, before returning home. Evangeline had broken the engagement with such cruel words that Laura was driven to a torrent of tears. How could her sister be so callous? How could she write to the man she professed to love that not only would there would be no wedding, she never wanted to see him again.

On arriving home, the news that Evangeline had left for

work at the hat shop hardened Laura's resolve. So, with a pile of Evangeline's beautifully decorated stationery, Laura fled to the privacy of her room, where in the comfort of her window seat, she proceeded to steal her sister's identity and replace the letter to Roger with one of her own composition. A far kinder and more compassionate message than the harsh breaking of the engagement. After all, Evangeline must surely regret her hasty decision and be grateful to Laura for intervening.

When she had finished her task, she wondered how she felt no guilt at her deception, only satisfaction. If the inevitability of consequences intruded into her thoughts, they had been quickly dismissed.

Roger Brown deserved better.

February 9, 1942
Vaucluse, NSW

Dear Charlotte,

I have done the most dreadful thing. I must confess to someone, and as my dearest friend in all the world I fear I have chosen you to bear my secret, knowing that however you may judge my actions, you will not abandon the closeness of our friendship.

I hope by the end of this letter that I have been able to traverse some way towards making you understand. Although I am not sure I understand my own actions, but know my heart to be true.

It is the kinship of our minds and the shared memories of our hearts that gives me courage to write to you. After all, one must have a true friend to whom one can unburden one's deepest thoughts. We have shared so many confidences that I know you will stand by me, and never reveal to a living soul the depths of my deception.

I will hold you in suspense no longer. My sister, Evangeline, who has just turned twenty, recently became engaged to a young soldier. He is British by birth and family but has joined the Australian infantry. On the day he was to leave to join his regiment, Evangeline wrote a letter to him, breaking off their engagement. She gave the letter into my hands to deliver it to the railway station.

I simply couldn't do it, Charlotte.

Instead, I wrote to him myself, as Evangeline, and now feel I must carry the charade. I feel sick at the thought, but can see no other course.

He was deployed to Europe. His location, of course, is secret. But all the indications in the newspapers seem to point to the possibility that he may be sent where the conflict is heaviest. It seemed inconceivable on the day of his leaving for me to accept the burden of handing him a letter that must surely crush his heart and ruin his future. My fears for his state of mind at this abandonment at such a terrible time caused me to undertake this rash course of action.

Oh, that Evangeline had the courage to handle it better! They had only known each other a matter of weeks. What was poor Roger Brown to know of her mercurial nature? She seemed in love with the idea of a man in uniform, but then she became morose and short with us all, bemoaning that her social life would now be at an end.

Even now, I cannot judge Evangeline harshly, especially in light of my own actions, which will surely bring me the harshest punishment of all, although I hold out hope that the matter will resolve itself.

Desperately yours, Laura.

Ps. Please do not abandon me in my hour of need!!!!

February 26, 1940
North Shore Hospital
Sydney

Dear Laura,

Oh Laura, you do get yourself into the most amazing scrapes! This time I fear you have outdone all your past adventures. Of course, I shall keep your confidence. I even smuggled this letter out of the house without the prying eyes of Miss Butterworth, our housekeeper. You remember her – she constantly spied on our every word when you last visited.

At least the war, as dreadful as it is, has opened doors. With all the hurry and bustle in the house with my two brothers enlisting no one notices me at all, a state I find much to my liking. I am positively bursting with good news. I have at last been able to persuade Papa to allow me to begin nurse training. He is closing down our Sydney house and moving to the hinterland with mother, Miss Butterworth and William.

William is greatly put out by this decision because some of his friends forged their birth certificates and other documents and were able to enlist at fourteen or fifteen. He was only consoled when he discovered that underage boys were promptly put to work peeling vegetables in the kitchens. He views the Armed Services in a different light.

Now he is moaning that the war will not last long enough.

I feel sure that you must receive communication from poor Roger Brown. It is a little too hopeful of you to think that a newly affianced man would forget the woman he loves.

At least in my new premises of the nurses' home I may receive mail without arousing the suspicions of family.

Poor you. I should not like to be the one to receive Evangeline's scorn. But how will you intercept the mail at home?

Surely Evangeline did not keep the engagement ring? That would be very bad form indeed, but as you didn't mention it, and knowing your sister, I can only assume that she hasn't seen fit to return it. What a turmoil to be in! To think of a poor soldier keeping his love's letter near his heart, only for her love to be false all the while.

I'm sure you will think of a way to write to Roger and find the words to tell him the truth of the situation. As cruel as it may be to have one's heart broken in pieces, it must eventually be better to know the whole. You may much time to consider the problem as I hear the mail to our soldiers is interminably slow.

However, I cannot share your optimism that the matter will resolve itself. I fear you may have to gather courage and out yourself!

I look forward to seeing you again!

Lovingly, Charlotte

May 3, 1942,
London

Dear Miss Evangeline Holden,

I thank you for your kind correspondence to my brother Roger. Your tender sentiments moved me greatly. My brother had not informed me of the engagement, but I had not expected him to do so. I'm afraid it has been many years since he confided in me.

Sadly, it falls to me to be the bearer of grim news. There's no getting around it and being a man of straightforward nature I will get on with it.

Even though I'm confident that you have received suitable correspondence from the armed services I feel the need to write to you myself, as the older brother of Roger, your affianced.

Roger was injured in the first battle where he encountered a barrage of shrapnel. I will spare you the worst details, but Roger is currently hospitalised in London. Some of the scars will heal, however the blindness is permanent and his mental state is fragile and the prognosis for that condition is uncertain.

I chose to keep him in London, rather than one of the rural rehabilitation facilities as I am currently employed in government offices here.

I realise that in Australia you are not unaware of the effects of war but nevertheless, this news will come as a shock.

However, I hasten to reassure you that Roger treasures your faithfulness and anticipates your letters with such delight that I have taken to reading them to him myself, rather than rely on the busy nurses. I must say that I also enjoy these correspondences, and am much amused by your Australian humour and somewhat naïve life observations. I assure you that I mean this last as a compliment.

Roger has expressed admiration for your tender concern, having felt on his departure that your affection for him might have abated. It seems that, for you, absence has made the heart grow fonder.

We look forward to further correspondence from you.

Yours, Elliot Brown.

June 19, 1942
Vaucluse, NSW

Dear Charlotte,

I am lost, utterly lost.

You will not believe the new circumstances of my predicament. I had steeled myself to write to Roger and explain all but I'm afraid it is now impossible. At least for the foreseeable future.

I received correspondence, not from Roger, but from his older brother Elliot, who in spite of his cordiality seems to be a person of some pomposity. I dare say it's due to the birthright of being the eldest, like our Evangeline.

He delivered the exceedingly bad news that Roger was blinded in battle and is presently incarcerated (is that the right word?) in some sort of mental institution. I am a shallow person indeed, for my sympathy for him has significantly waned. Not only because of his terrible injuries and state of mind but because I had a long visit with Evangeline.

She had written me the dearest note of such tender affection that I forgot my vow to cut her off and hastened to her side. There she revealed, with many tears and sniffling howls, that Roger had hit her and that was the reason for the breaking of the engagement. I had no choice to believe her as the bruising, although greatly faded, was unmistakable.

Of course, I confessed all to her, but rather than sympathise with my predicament she laughed excessively and claimed I had cheered her immensely.

However, when I applied to her for assistance, she merely said, 'You're on your own there, little sister.'

Evangeline refused to even conjure any advice and called upon her roommate, Cynthia to join in what she referred to the hilarious capers of her silly sister.

I should have been insulted but it was so good to be reconciled to her, and she did conjure up a superior afternoon tea. Cynthia is training as a sous chef so Evangeline's pleas for me to return often were more than welcome.

The renewal of our sisterly affection was greatly restored by the reassurance given by Evangeline that she will not convey one word of our conversation to our parents.

Meanwhile, I feel I have no other choice than to continue with the deception for the time being, which means more letter writing. It may ameliorate the situation to write from here on to both brothers. Elliot, the elder Brown, states that he receives mail at a more secure and reliable rate than his brother.

Still desperately yours, Laura.

June 30, 1942
Vaucluse, NSW

Dear brothers Grimm,

You must pardon my cheek in calling you that as it seems every letter I receive brings more bad news.

Dear Elliot - I am exceedingly sorry that Roger has experienced such trouble adjusting to his blindness. I thought my letters would cheer him enough to convince him to allow the nurses to take him outside.

I shall suppress the impulse to give him a sound telling off as I am sure the staff has already done so.

I am grateful to you, *Elliot Brown*, for taking over the communication due to Roger's penchant for pitching a fit over any part of my letters that aggravates him.

It must be galling to live in blurred darkness and if my accounts of a livelier life are egregiously cursed by him at times then I cannot apologise for my letters would be sad missives indeed if I wrote only of boring matters.

I had thought to cheer him by my stories and accounts of life here, but nevertheless…

He must surely appreciate your care of him, Elliot, for it is remarkably steadfast and earnest.

I certainly appreciate your promise to omit anything from your reading to Roger that might upset him, although I fear that must leave very little on occasion.

I apologise for the smudge on my signature on my last letter. However, it is my turn to be completely frank with you, and by that I am addressing Elliot. Again.

Now for my long overdue confession. It is not Evangeline but I, Laura, who has been writing to you. I'm afraid my naivety and wilful nature has pushed me to interfere in my sister's life in an alarming way.

There is no excuse for this lapse in judgement but I hope you will view me somewhat kindly as my intentions were honourable, at least I thought they were at the time.

On the evening of Roger's departure Evangeline pressed a letter into my hands with the strict instructions to deliver it to Roger at Central Station.

It is perhaps fortunate that Roger remembers so little of his time here in Australia but I suppose this is due to his mental state, which you tell me is in decline rather badly.

I have visited my sister Evangeline and my regret and humiliation with regard to my actions increased one hundred fold. She has forgiven me, which action I hope you will follow. As for Roger, you must do as you wish. I am at your mercy, and deserve to be.

May 3, 1942,
London

Dear Usurper

Please forgive my "cheek" in calling you that, Laura, but I cannot contain my amusement at your deception. I shudder to think what could have happened…

I must admit to a certain degree of trepidation. You see Roger has quite the reputation with the ladies, and not a reputation that any man of good stature would aspire to possessing.

But enough of that. I just say that I did suspect some game afoot. I wasn't sure exactly what game, but when Roger muttered that Evangeline must have had a conversion of sorts, I headed in the direction of subterfuge.

It was not unexpected for someone to fudge the truth in order to gain access to our family.

Of course, I now realise that you, LAURA, are blissfully unaware of our status in good old England. We Brits tend to forget that the colonies deem us as irrelevant, if not boring.

Roger showed no surprise when I notified him of your identity. His mercurial nature has already fixed on another target for his affections. A lamentable trait that has been long cultivated and honed. A nurse of course. He never hunts far from home.

I apologise for speaking in this manner but I feel that I must be real with you, and indeed, with your sister Evangeline, who quite possibly had ascertained Roger's true nature.

On my part, dear Laura, all is forgiven and I do hope you will continue to correspond. I'm at a loss as to how I will otherwise entertain the nurses on my visits to my brother.

Yours, Elliot.

PS: I was also aware of your subterfuge when Roger received the engagement ring by registered post not long after your first letter.

You cannot imagine my relief on receiving your last letter. I had been in a flurry of anxiety ever since my confession. Nay, before that. Soon after I undertook to substitute myself in my sister's place, in fact.

I should have known that I would sound much different from Evangeline, but I thought that as she and Roger had spent so little time together before their engagement that I would get away with it. Silly me.

How shocked I was to discover that you knew my perfidy earlier. It was too bad of you to let me carry on like a loon, but I suppose I deserve no other response.

Evangeline has proved to be the most forgiving of sisters. Although I feel that her ire has been ameliorated by the entertainment value she has made the most of, on every available occasion to place me as the butt of the joke.

I dare say the sting will wear off and I shall tell the story with great amusement to my future grandchildren. But for now, I am sunk in humiliation.

My best friend Charlotte is to graduate from her nurse training. I don't know how she does it. When I last visited her the whole place was in an uproar because one of the dementia patients had gone missing. He was found later, completely soused at the local pub. The bartender had served him in spite of his name being written across the seat of his pants in bold lettering – an attempt to have him recognised as a patient if he wandered. The gig was up when he tried to pay with Monopoly money.

I was so put out by your revelation in your postscript that I grabbed a piece of plain paper as it was the closest to hand. I also omitted to add address and date.

I can't believe that a year has passed since I first wrote.

Yours, the Usurper.

PS: I have gained possession of some London society pages. Apparently, you, sir, are London's most eligible bachelor. I see that British newspapers write the same kind of rot as our colonial papers.

June 20, 1942
Vaucluse, NSW

Dear Charlotte,

I have been compelled to confess all to the Brown brothers. It was the only thing I could do. As you know I am a truly unimaginative liar. I had run out of ridiculous explanations and attempting to sound like Evangeline who is a great deal more worldly than I.

The older, Brown, Elliot had known all along which I thought him a poor sport to continue, but I know it is only what I deserve.

I have decided that nursing is not the career for me so I won't be joining you in nurse training. Instead, I have taken on an editing apprenticeship of sorts with the local rag, hoping to eventually gain entrance to the hallowed ground of a major newspaper publication. It was a definite bonus that we undertook that Pittman's typing course as I'm sure it helped me greatly to gain my current employment, although I would have turned up for the job without pay.

I hope we will be able to catch up regularly in spite of my defection to the world of scribbling.

I have used up Evangeline's floral writing paper. She has refused to lend me more so I shall have to resort to plain old white paper from now on as the money I receive from the paper will not cover such extravagances.

Yours, Laura.

I can't tell you how much your letters amuse and entertain me. Of course, I read them in their entirety before taking them to my brother.

He is now married to the sweet little nurse who gave him such tender care in the rehabilitation facility. This, of course, means that I will now have two "children" to supervise.

I am, however, pleased to find that my new sister-in-law is made of sterner stuff than I first thought.

I'm fascinated by your reference to grandchildren. How many of those do you intend on having? If they have your sassy nature I believe that more than a dozen would be too great a challenge to undertake.

You are right to assume that London newspapers write "rot". I am certainly not London's most eligible bachelor. That title belongs to the Honourable Jeremy Blethington who has a substantial fortune, is a Member of Parliament and owns, not one, but two country estates as well as his London apartments. If you wish a introduction, I will be happy to arrange that small service. He is a fastidious writer of letters, however, most of them are strident letters of criticism of members of the opposition.

Yours, London's least eligible bachelor

PS: I am impressed by your use of plain paper and will forthwith write on any old piece of paper that crosses my path. How liberating.

How dare you suggest that I would not manage more than a dozen grandchildren. I am deeply offended by your unfair assessment of my grandparenting abilities. I'm sure I could manage any number of grandchildren. I have loads of experience with infants. Evangeline has two very active toddlers and I manage both very well thank you.

Add to that the three nephews that my brothers have provided and I'm practically an expert.

Can you believe that two years have passed. There is much speculation about the end of the war, but as the pundits vowed it would be over by Christmas in 1940 I remain cynical.

I have moved into a flat with my friend Charlotte. This arrangement won't last long as I am to be her bridesmaid in a few months. I feel that I have joined the circus, such are the demands on a matron of honour. I have decided to elope if I am ever tempted to enter marriage.

Charlotte is altogether changed and begging far and wide for extra ration cards, yards of satin and suitable dressmakers. The only part of that malarky has been the cake testing, which was so satisfying I could almost change my mind about elopement.

Father has put a damper on that idea by saying that he finds the prospect of my eloping to give him great satisfaction. There is nothing that spurs a girl to do the opposite when a parent unexpectedly agrees with one's ideas.

I have gained employment as a sub-editor for the Sydney Morning Herald and look forward to writing a great deal of rot. However, at present I am limited to the Obituary Column.

I hope to climb up the ladder and someday write about the living, but for the moment I am satisfied.

I was extraordinarily pleased when I was chosen to write a piece on wedding cakes. However, my pleasure was dimmed when my name was not attached to said piece. Apparently that's par for the course.

Yours, Laura.

PS: Speaking of grandchildren, how many do YOU intend on having? And … by the by … how was it that your letter was postmarked from Sydney??

Dear Laura,

Yes, I am in Sydney. A man can hardly propose to a woman from thousands of miles away. This is something I intend to do in person. Shall you be available next week? Or tomorrow?

Yours hopefully, Elliot

Taken

'Come on, Delia. Keep up!' Eric Branson wheedled.

'I'm not … arrgh.' Georgia groaned softly. Visiting her father was getting harder with each visit. Today she was his wife. She followed him down the nursing home corridor.

Georgia had a lot of time for her sister-in-law Judith, but going along with each new delusion was one area where they didn't see eye to eye. However, one did not argue with Judith. She had that smooth way of overlooking what you said while carrying on with the conversation. *Her* conversation. A social worker, Judith was the accepted expert and ignored other opinions as one would a blip on the radar of life.

Eric's mind was deteriorating faster than his body. Keeping up with his loping strides across the large recreation area of the nursing home was difficult, especially when he would stop abruptly to sweet talk one of the kitchen staff or nurses on his way.

Georgia waited patiently during these interludes. She honestly didn't mind—it meant less time alone with him. Less time to be regaled with his disappointments with life, or whoever he thought her to be at the time.

His smile and generous air were a gift not often bestowed

on his own family. She supposed she should have been pained by the universally mourned changes in her father like everyone else, but Georgia could see little difference in his personality. Her father's diagnosis with Alzheimer's had not rocked her world nearly as much as the loss of her beloved mother when she was 16.

'Come on, Angel,' murmured Eric.

Georgia resisted the urge to burst out laughing. She'd never heard her father call anyone 'angel'. Perhaps he thought he was in Heaven today. However, the tirade he released when they reached the privacy of his room, suggested *not*.

'I can't believe you're leaving me and travelling halfway around the world to teach some foreign women how to use a sewing machine. What am I to you? Nothing?'

Confused, Georgia opened her mouth to respond, but Eric Branson was not done yet.

'Thought you'd sneak off and not tell me did you? Well, thank goodness for Judith. So like you, to let someone else drop the bombshell.'

'I... you...' Georgia stumbled over her words while her brain tried to catch up. An affect her father always had on her. One thing was becoming clear, her father knew who she was today, the day she had come to let him know of her plans. She'd come straight from the travel agent the volunteer agency had organised the visit through.

'I'm here to tell you today. I just came from the...'

'You think I'm stupid, don't you. You must have been planning this for months. Couldn't tell me before, hey? I had to hear it from someone else, not my own child.' He paced the room, his rage as towering as his height.

Georgia was furious. He had everything wrong. She stood. Her mother had told her that she needed to learn to 'stick up' for herself. Never mind 'not upsetting mentally impaired' patients. Never mind being the glue that held her father together. Stuff it all.

'You have no right, Dad...'

'I'm glad your mother isn't alive to see this,' said Eric.

Turning on her heel, Georgia picked up her handbag and walked out the door. She heard a primal roar as her shoes clipped out a staccato rhythm down the hall.

'Oh dear,' said Jeanette, the head nurse, as she lay a gentle hand on Georgia's arm. 'We do understand, you know. He's like this with us.'

Georgia's eyes were round with shock, 'Really?'

'Yes, lovey. They can't hide much here. It sounds like a Class One Tantrum.'

Georgia smiled as tears threatened. 'Is that what you write in his notes?'

'Not likely.' Jeanette winked. Doesn't stop us having our own code.' She paused to listen. 'I wonder if he'll need medicating to calm down.'

'I might,' murmured Georgia.

Jeanette let out a cracking laugh. 'You and me both, lovey. You and me both.'

Georgia leaned against the corridor wall. She needed to calm down. She couldn't leave like this. She'd drive like a maniac. Cry like a waterfall, or something.

'What's this all about then, young Eric?' she heard Jeanette address her father. The answer was childlike, small. Georgia strained to listen. Was that her father's voice?

She heard footsteps. Large clunking ones. Soft nurses' shoes. She withdrew behind the linen trolley.

'Sorry Sister, Mum wouldn't let my play outside,' said Eric. 'But you will, won't you sweetie. You're my pet.' He linked his arm through Jeanette's and stumbled along. Georgia had been told her father's changes could be sudden, but nothing prepared her for this.

'Did you enjoy the visit with your daughter?' asked Jeanette.

Eric laughed and gave her his most charming smile. 'Oh, you are such a tease, sweetie. I'm not even married. Young buck like me. You do love to wind a fella up.'

Tears slipped slowly down Georgia's cheeks as she carefully read and re-read the shipping notice. She had already packed the boxes of fabrics and haberdashery with minute care. It didn't need to be done again, but she couldn't help checking. The electric sewing machines and other dressmaking aids had already been shipped.

Swiping the tears with the back of her hand meant taking off her glasses every few seconds.

She despised the tears without wanting to delve into the reasons for them. It wasn't just her father's reaction. Her brother Paul had left no doubts that he was against the trip, as was his wife. Lunacy, that was the word he'd used. 'You might as well by going alone, Georgia. You don't know anyone there. You've never met this Brian bloke. Some arrogant Yank.'

It sounded more like his wife, Judith, but then Georgia was

never sure if her brother was speaking his own mind, or that of his wife.

Finally, placing her glasses carefully aside, she signed the forms, attached them to the large box.

And this was how Eve found Georgia an hour later.

Eve's cool hand on her forehead was the catalyst to a further rush of scalding tears. Cradled in her friend's arms the wrench of her heartache subsided quickly.

'Remind me again why I gave you a key to my house?' said Georgia with mock severity as she wiped her face with the handkerchief Eve offered.

'Did you visit your father?'

'Yes. Sometimes I think you're psychic.'

'It's not rocket science. Every time you visit him, it's the same.'

'Please tell me you didn't tell him where you were going!'

'No, I just said I would be away for a while, but he knew. Someone told him.'

Eve rolled her eyes. 'He gets to you doesn't he.'

'But sometimes he's... different.'

'Different/same, it doesn't matter. Your response is always the same. He's pushed your buttons for so long it's instinctive for him even without his marbles.'

'It's rotten timing. I wanted to leave for Pakistan in peace.'

'Your father is a man who has called the shots for 70 years. He's never going to become meek as an angel. Goodbyes are hard enough for happy people, and your father has never been happy.'

'That's not what the world thinks.'

'The world is an ass.'

'I thought the law was an ass.'

'Oh, there's room for all kinds of asses in this world.'

Georgia chuckled. 'You are such a sweet friend. How was I ever lucky enough to find you?'

'We found each other.'

Reaching for the travel guide she realised that Eve's visit had lifted her spirits.

She looked at the clock on the wall. 11.15 am. A moan escaped her lips. She had thought her last day in Australia before travelling would be a flurry of activity.

Trust her to be so organised that there wasn't a thing to do but worry. Bad enough that her father had decided to have one of his moods, it certainly didn't help the tight knot of anxiety over being a first-time overseas traveller at the ripe old age of thirty.

Flipping the pages in a desultory fashion, Georgia settled into the soft corduroy lounge. A white furry tail flicked her face as Zeke, feline queen of the domain stalked along the back of the three-seater before settling under Georgia's chin.

'Great, thanks Zeke, now I can't even see the pamphlet.'

Zeke took this admonishment as the highest of compliments and splayed her body across Georgia, purring with satisfaction.

Georgia sighed and put the pamphlet down. She didn't intend doing much sightseeing anyway, and the warmth and contentment of another being was soporific. The morning had shuffled along at a maddening pace. It was too early for lunch.

'I hope I have a decent travel companion, Zeke.'

After twisting the sheets into knots until the early hours, sleep softly claimed her.

In an upmarket Los Angeles restaurant the house music was low, making it easier for a sleek young woman to be heard by her fiancé. 'I'm just not getting through to you, am I Brian?' Ann asked, her head tilted to one side.

'Do you know how cute you look when you give me your teacher look? Shall I do detention? Write a page of the dictionary? A Shakespearean sonnet? Oh, I know, one of Robert Blake's...'

A tear formed in the corner of Ann's eye. Brian leaned in to wipe it away, but Ann stopped him with a raised hand. The gesture was so guarded that it stopped him in his tracks. Ann was never like this. What had gotten into her?

'Sweetheart, I'm sorry I'm being light-hearted. I just wanted to make our goodbyes easier. But I won't be gone long. I'm doing it for you.'

Ann's eyes flashed angrily. '*For me?* You're going halfway across the world as a volunteer in some third world country *for me?*'

'I'm trying to show you I'm capable of responsibility. Ready to settle down. That's what you wanted wasn't it? I thought you realised I was taking on this experience to prove that to you.'

'Ann folded her arms. 'You just don't get it, do you, Brian?'

'Well, I would, if you'd just explain it to me. You said you wanted commitment. I gave you a ring, you said you wanted maturity. I've kept my job. You said you wanted depth and... the other thing, compassion. What more can I do? I've put everything on the line for you.'

'You've what? I can't believe what I'm hearing. I've supported you through broken promises, "demanding job" that you couldn't handle, past girlfriends showing up that you said meant nothing...'

'You gave me an ultimatum, Ann.'

Ann's face flushed. 'I gave you a choice, Brian. There's a huge difference.'

'If this is a play on words I don't understand. It's the same thing. You've changed, you always said you liked my Peter Pan boyishness.'

Ann brushed a tear from her cheek. 'You're lying Brian. You left your job weeks ago. I'm done.'

Brian reached for her hand across the table. 'Babe...'

Withdrawing her hand, Ann removed the engagement ring. Taking Brian's hand gently she placed the ring there and folded his fingers around it.

'What the...'

'Tick, tock.' Ann's voice trembled.

'Ann, now you're scaring me. What...'

'I'm sorry Peter Pan, but I'm choosing the crocodile. I'm not Wendy. This isn't Neverland.'

Ann's steps faltered as she turned and walked away.

'Why the hell am I going to Pakistan for three months?' Brian said to Anne's retreating back.

Ann's steps quickened, ringing louder and stronger.

Brian swore as he realised the diners around him were

staring. He ordered another bottle of wine and a decadent dessert. By the time he was halfway through both, he was more cheerful. Anne would come back. She always did. He would go on this crazy charity gig, and win her back.

'And why pray tell, am I taking you to the airport little brother?' asked Enrico.

'I'd rather not talk about it... In fact I'd rather not talk at all,' muttered Brian as he threw his Luis Vuitton suitcase into his brother's car.

'Ah, my favourite state of grace, you not speaking. I shall be able to indulge in a rare journey of Wagner.'

Brian slammed the boot shut.

'Mind the vehicle, Echo,' said Enrico.

Brian winced on hearing his childhood pet name. He clenched his teeth. 'Don't call me that! You don't know what I've been through.'

'And I don't want to, so we have harmony – for once.'

'I thought Italians were hot-headed.' Brian slung the words at his half-brother. A fight with anyone would be better than the pain he felt after breaking up with Ann.

'Ah, but I'm only half Italian.'

'Does that make you lukewarm, then?'

'My dear Echo, you have known me for all of your 28 years and not once have you been able to goad me. Why try now?'

Enrico steered the sedan effortlessly into the stream of cars heading through the city.

Brian moaned. Even the traffic parted for Enrico the Great, he thought. His immaculate brother had probably descended from Moses. It galled him that Enrico had... what was it Ann said... gravitas.

Damn Ann, he hadn't seen that coming. What timing, to break up mere hours before his flight.

'You're just like Ann.' Brian spat the words.

'Why thank you, a compliment. You're improving.'

'You don't have to be so patronising.'

'But I do. I changed your nappy. That gives me a lifetime right to condescend.'

'It's not written in stone that because you are the oldest that you can treat me like a child for the rest of my life.'

'So, are you telling me that you intend to stop acting like a child for the rest of your life? That is good news. I felicitate you on your coming of age.'

Brian let loose a string of expletives. 'You're not even the head of the family. You're not even Dad's son. You're a wog. You think you run this family... Ann's broken it off with me. There does that make you happy? Maybe you want her for yourself. Two of the same. Always in control, you might call it self-control, but I know it's really controlling everything and everyone. You're the same as her. Nothing's ever good enough.'

Enrico's hands tightened on the wheel, his eyes slits of steel. Silence reigned. The concerto waned, the string section lilting softly, as if to calm the two men. The oboe was low and sonorous.

Brian swallowed, anger pushing him to the edge, bitter and all consuming. 'Just because my father married your whoring mother before he married mine...'

The car swung to the side of the road. Enrico killed the

engine. 'Get out,' he said, turning to face his blonde brother. 'Now.'

'You...'

'Do not mistake me in this.' Enrico removed the keys and held them near his shoulder, eyes hard as black coal.

Brian froze. 'Go to hell!'

'If you do not exit the vehicle I will come around and assist you in every way I can.' Enrico jiggled the keys.

'What about my...'

Enrico pressed the keypad. The sound of the boot popping open shocked Brain into action.

'What about my flight? Really! I've been under a lot of stress.'

'Do shut the door gently, Echo. We both know you won't be on that plane. You're a coward.'

Brian stepped back from the shoulder of the road. The traffic was slewing gravel, stinging his legs. He flicked the handle of the suitcase open. Not one of these commuters would give him the time of day, much less a lift anywhere. A horn parped, making him jump back. He couldn't remember feeling so alone.

Looking around he tried to get his bearings. Fixing his eyes on the nearest highway exit, he realised he was a mile or more from the airport. He could walk to the exit and then get a taxi. Then what? Angrily he began to stride out the distance. By the time he reached the exit and saw a telephone booth, his anger had been replaced by exhaustion. He phoned a taxi. He'd think of a destination when the taxi came. He sat on the suitcase, not wishing to face the onlookers at the local takeaway. The taxi arrived in minutes.

Brian stood and gripped the suitcase.

'Where to, Sir?'

'JFK. The airport. International terminal.'

On the other side of the world, Georgia was checking in at Sydney Kinsgsford Smith Airport. She willed the tight knot of tension in her stomach to retreat. There was no need to worry, she'd double checked everything.

Her mobile rang. Muffled by the din of travellers and staff, she didn't hear it at first. Diving into her handbag, she found it easily. It was Judith, sister-in-law and dispense of advice. Georgia's fingers hovered over the screen.

'Flight K362 for Pakistan now boarding,' announced the loudspeaker.

Georgia hesitated, watching as the blinking light on the phone faded, then died. Judith. She sighed. Next would come the ping of the message box. Better than the long list of "things to worry about" from Ms Fix-It, who had never fixed anything this side of the country.

'Here's your boarding pass, Madam. Have a good flight,' said the smiling girl at the desk.

Georgia returned the girl's smile with a nervous flinch. There wasn't much chance of that... unless... Eyeing the phone as if it was a living dangerous thing she pressed the off button.

Georgia didn't meet Brian until three days into her stay. She had been busy setting up the machines and meeting the local women, whose charm had enchanted her from the moment she had been introduced to them. Some were very young, some older, but all had a habit of shy giggling behind their hijabs.

While her role was clear, when Brian arrived he seemed lost. He found the accents of the local men hard to understand. It was his role to help with woodturning, but he constantly complained about the tools and the heat.

Georgia only saw Brian when the staff met for the evening meal, when the women had hurried home to their families. The meals were later than Georgia was accustomed, but she loved the food.

After the meal, she and Brian were picked up by a local and taken through the streets of Abbottabad in the rattling old station wagon of Hamza, the CEO of the charity, a chatty Pakistani who wove stories of his hometown as he drove, one hand on the wheel.

It was growing dark. Georgia wrapped her Shalwar Kameez around her. She had opted to wear the traditional clothing. After three weeks in Abbottabad Georgia had become accustomed to the street.

It was too quiet. Hamza was late. Then, the sound of shouting erupted in a nearby street. dark vehicles with men hanging out of the Ute trays swirled dust at the end of the street. One broke away, a more expensive sleek vehicle.

Georgia slunk into the shadows of the building. Where was Hamza? What was happening?

A roar, yelling, breathless, hessianed-darkness as a sac is thrown over her head and secured. Screaming, endless screaming, then a sting. Georgia feels Brian struggle.

Georgia fought blackness as they are bundled into a dark AWD. On awakening from a drug induced haze, terror claimed her. In a dark, cramped room echoes of her childhood intrude. Her father's rages. Hiding from him.

Brian paced the room like a caged animal, tearing long fingers through blonde dishevelled hair. It was clear now. They had been kidnapped. God only knows why, in this country of madness and conflict.

There must be some mistake. He and Georgia were volunteers. What would anyone gain by holding them hostage? He tried to find somewhere to sit. He didn't want to wake Georgia. She had been awake and trembling for two days. The dark room offered little light, but he found the crumbling step by the door, and sank onto it.

Then, realising that he was next to the only entrance and would be knocked flying if their captors decided to open the door, he crossed the room blindly and slumped in a corner. He didn't need any more bruises or cuts.

There was an ancient sack there, smelling of canine presence. With a chill he realised it was probably one of the bags that had been thrown over their heads as they had been snatched and hurled into the back of the Hummer. What irony. To be stolen away in America's favourite car by dissidents who hated them.

What would happen to them? What would they do to Georgia—a woman in a strange land? Would it make any difference that she was Australian? As bargaining chips they were pretty poor fodder. Had they been mistaken for some other target? High ranking officials or corporate capitalist enemies?

It had all happened so quickly.

By the time Georgia came to, Brian had gained some perspective. His family was wealthy. Enrico could get his hands on a fortune. His brother may hold the key to their release. He knew Enrico. He would never leave his brother, no matter how much they fought.

'A lot of these things are to fund terrorism,' he told Georgia.

'Things?'

'Ransoms from Westerners fund their ... activities.'

Georgia croaked an awkward scoffing sound. 'I have no funds. They chose badly with me.'

Two weeks passed with food slipped through a slit in the door, removed for this purpose.

'The food is good,' said Georgia. 'That's a good sign, don't you think?'

Brian shrugged.

A child cried. Georgia stirred, wrapping the dark blanket around her she sat on the edge of the bed that was fraying hessian strapped to ancient metal struts.

An old woman's voice filtered through the door. She was soothing a child. There was the sound of metal clattering, pots and pans. They must be next to the kitchen. The old woman sang, then let out a single gravelly word that sounded like a curse.

The door opened. Neither Brian nor Georgia moved. The old woman pushed a saucepan with two spoons towards them and gestured for them to remain where they were, ending with a throat cutting motion.

The woman's eyes were fierce, but Georgia also sensed fear. The men had left her to guard them, as well as care for a small child. She stood for a moment as if mesmerised by Georgia. Georgia was watching her, with only her green eyes visible through the blanket.

In that frozen instant the child ran towards Georgia, throwing himself at her with a torrent of words. The old woman sucked in a terrified breath. Horrifying moments passed. Even the air in the room was heavy. Seconds ticked by on a knife edge. It was an impossible situation.

Georgia held the child. It was a boy, no more than two. Smiling tentatively she soothed him, never taking her eyes from the woman. The boy must have mistaken her for part of the family.

Turning him around gently she pointed towards the woman, who came to life and beckoned him with her arms waving. The child toddled towards the door. Relief showed on the old woman's face, but she let out a stream of angry words and slammed the door.

'Oh dear God, that was close,' said Brian. 'I swear she was looking into your soul.'

'Perhaps she was,' said Georgia.

'Well, we're as good as dead now.'

'I don't know. That woman could be our salvation.'

Through the second-storey window of his construction company, Paul Collins, Georgia's brother chewed the end of his draftsmen's pencil and glared down at the group of reporters jostling outside his office.

He should have known something like this would happen to his sister. He'd never known anyone to get in this much trouble as his younger sibling. She was a magnet for it, in spite of all her protestations that she only wanted a peaceful life.

Janice, his nervous secretary had, for once in her bumbling life, done the right thing and locked the door, more likely out of fear than any careful strategy.

For a brief distracted moment he stared at the pencil. It had been decades since he'd mangled a pencil down to a mere inch, a habit he'd developed in his teens to annoy his mother, a domineering woman who stood guard over his bedroom while he sat at his desk and made little pretence of actually doing his homework. They had a well-established afternoon ritual where he chewed pencils instead of even opening a schoolbook while his mother bemoaned the waste of good pencils and the diminishing future prospects of the son and heir. The whole exercise afforded Paul a good deal of quiet satisfaction and annoyed the hell out of his mother.

So overbearing was his mother that she had woken him the day before his wedding and ordered him to get a haircut. For once he'd accommodated her. After all, he was escaping female domination, a theory that was sorely tested when his new bride-to-be had begun a tirade that lasted the entire rehearsal, late into the night and began again when the photographer arrived for the ceremony. The prospect of several weeks of undisturbed hot sex with Judith who'd already demonstrated an eagerness for passion in the bedroom pushed aside any niggling doubt that perhaps he'd married a prototype of his mother.

A sleek BMW swept into the carpark. Thank God Judith had arrived. He had no idea how to deal with media attention. Trust his bloody chaotic sister to get herself in another spectacular mess. He'd just received the phone call from the police telling him that Georgia had been kidnapped in Pakistan with another misguided aid worker, some computer geek whose wealthy American family had already given a press conference and were negotiating payment with the kidnappers.

Paul realised he would have to speak to the press at some stage. Feign anxiety and concern. He hadn't approved of this trip and he had been right. They weren't close. His condescending disdain for her messy divorce hadn't helped their relationship. Now Georgia was in Pakistan on a two week junket helping set up a small dressmaking cooperative for a group of village women while Damien was visiting his father in Hong Kong. God knows how Georgia had managed to talk her ex, Dan, in to taking their son for any length of time, the guy showed more interest in his new wife's shoe collection than his own child. At least there'd be no custody battle.

But this last thought brought a terrifying new aspect to the crisis. He and Judith had agreed to raise Dylan if anything happened to Georgia. Ye gods, why had they smiled benignly and signed off on that!—the things one says and does for family, never imagining … praying … . Dylan, who was only bearable in small doses and showed all the energy and anarchism of a budding terrorist.

Paul checked his tie in the mirror and wished he'd decided to work on a building site that day, somewhere where his affluence was less apparent. With a hard hat and overalls that would leave kidnappers with the impression he didn't have a razoo to spare and wasn't worth their negotiations.

He'd better front the media. He was, after all, Georgia's only relative. With their father demented and in a nursing home, he was left to deal with it.

He met Judith outside the lift. She reassured him with a tight-lipped smile. With an arm under hers, he left the building where Judith paused briefly, removed her sunglasses with a confident flourish, and informed the clamouring press they were doing everything in their power to work with the relevant authorities to secure the release of Paul's sister.

They watched the news together over a bottle of Riesling, declaring the Davises, the family of the other hostage to be laying it on a little thick, with the Italian stepmother sobbing throughout the interview, an olive-skinned older son laying a hand on her shoulder while the father gazed shell-shocked past the cameras and vowed to pay any price for the return of his beloved youngest son, a gentle peacemaker.

Judith was pleased when the segment cut to her. Her round clipped tones were a little louder, a little more forceful than she'd thought, and she didn't remember saying that 'one should never negotiate with terrorists' before putting on her designer sunglasses, with the camera panning to her yelling at Paul to 'get in the car' then taking the wheel and smoothly driving out of the carpark with their heavily tinted windows closed.

Judith was stunned when the droll tones of a curious onlooker could be heard declaring 'that's one cold, hard bitch right there, that is. That poor sister will be headless before sunset, mark my words, mate.'

Enrico Davis stood outside the US embassy. The gleaming glass panelling glowed amber in the morning light. Like Georgia before him, he had been stunned by the colour and noise of the streets. Business had taken him all over the world, but nothing had prepared him for Pakistan. However, he could not afford to be caught up in the sights, sounds or colours.

He hesitated at the back of a growing media crowd, silently watching. Surely, they hadn't heard of Brian's escape with the girl. The news of Brian's kidnapping had made all the US papers, and the same must have applied in Australia about the girl from what Enrico could glean. The embassy had promised discretion until both had been medically examined and settled into a hotel with a flight organised.

He hesitated before leaving, hoping for a tidbit of information. The press weren't exactly a silent mob.

'They got him, *him*, can you believe it! Bin Laden,' said a suited man to his lanky cameraman. Enrico listened carefully, inching closer to the two.

'I know you'd like a scoop mate, but nothing's been confirmed. And with something this big we won't get details until every 'i' has been dotted and 't' crossed,' volunteered the cameraman.

'Yeah, well, you wouldn't know. I've been on this job longer than you. And we're staying put.'

'Suits me.' The cameraman lowered himself to sit cross legged on the lawn and took a long drag on his cigarette.

'Sir...' said one of the soldiers, moving forward slightly and gesturing at the cigarette.

'Right, sure.' The cameraman shoved the cigarette into the grass. 'I'm just saying. Any news this big will be notified from the White House by the President. That's where the scoop will be.'

Enrico flinched. This didn't sound right. But if it was, it meant the media circus wasn't here for news of the kidnapping, and that suited him just fine. The longer, the better.

'This will do for me. If they really have shot and killed Osama bin Laden, hearing it here will be big enough for me, especially if it turns out to be true. I can't see any rumours starting on anything this important without some shred of truth to it.'

Military police with spread-legged stance and eyes like passive slate lined the front of the building. Their silent vigil deterred the jostle and noise of the reporters cramped onto the front lawn. They would ask no questions of these men.

'Mr Davis.' A military attaché with quiet voice and subtle gestures approached Enrico and ushered him into the building through a rear entrance.

Pent up with anxiety and anticipation Enrico prowled the reception area. If he had been expecting the embassy to provide a quiet oasis, he was wrong. Scanning the room quickly he wondered how he would find Peter Brinton, the liaison diplomat who he'd spoken to on the phone. With a bleak smile that belied his impatience, Enrico decided to sit down in an alcove behind some tall green leafy plants. Where was Brian? And the woman who'd been kidnapped with him?

Brian and Georgia were awakened by loud voices. There was a clammer in the house, rustling kitchen activity, then a rich male voice. In the distance, the sound of fireworks.

The door swung open. The woman ushered them into a sitting room, where a tall man paced. 'Please sit,' he said.

Georgia slumped to the floor, but was bidden to rise and sit on a chair.

'This is most …disappointing.' The man paused. 'I have only the stupidity of my younger brothers to blame for this unfortunate event.' His voice was calm, there was gravitas missing from the younger men's voices.

'Listen carefully please. I am Moussad, that is all I will tell you of this time and place. I wish to resolve this incident, now tonight, with the least amount of … fuss. I can never undo the pain caused by my brothers but I will do my best. I will drive you tonight to the American Embassy. It is too difficult to get to the other … Australian?'

Georgia nodded.

'I have phoned them and your brother will be there. We must leave soon. There is unrest on the streets.'

The man stood. 'You must come now. I will ask you to wear blindfolds. I apologise for this but I cannot have focus on this house, my mother and sisters, you understand.'

He pressed a small fabric bag into each of their hands.

Brian thanked him, softly, voice weary with relief.

Georgia accepted, confused.

'You are a silent one,' Moussad said to Georgia. 'A woman without voice. Come. We go now.'

Georgia leaned back in the seat of the luxury car, profoundly grateful that they hadn't endured the sacs over the heads, hoping this showed that they were being taken where Moussad had said, rather than the outskirts to a camp, a video and a sword.

It was a swift journey that ended at the back of a building. Blindfolds removed, the doors were opened. It was not the Embassy.

Moussad spoke. 'This is as close as I go. Across the street. There. There is an official waiting.'

Georgia could see a man, but stiffness and apprehension stopped her from running across the street.

There were two men in the shadows. Brian threw himself at one of the men and the other man approached Georgia. They were ushered into the American Embassy.

'Thank God for you, Enrico.' Brian blathered, relief loosening his tongue. 'I knew you'd come through for me. And … Georgia's brother, of course.'

'Sit down Echo. The shock will hit you soon.'

Brian sat, warmed by his brother's smile. 'We're not related you know,' Brian said, 'his mother married my father before my mother did, but still this stellar man secured our release.'

The Embassy official cleared his throat. 'Not Quite Mr Davis. No funds were given for your release, although I must say that your brother has been in touch every day, sometimes more than once. It appears that your captors brought you back willingly without any funds exchanged.'

Enrico shrugged.

The official continued, 'As for you Ms Stone. Your brother…'

'Yes.?

Stay in your seat please. This is not good news for you, I'm afraid. Your brother obtained power of attorney and sold your house, ostensibly…'

'House? Ostensibly? What does that mean?' Georgia felt a hand on her shoulder. It was Brian's brother, who had quietly crossed the room to her side. Rather than comfort, the gesture seemed ominous.

'It appears that Mr Paul Collins has deposited the money in his own account, which in itself is not illegal, but he resisted attempts to explain himself to Mr Enrico here.'

'You saw him? He … What?'

Enrico came to stand in front of her. 'You can't get your house back, but you should have your brother charged if the money isn't transferred to you. His wife was there. She's a right one. I don't think … never mind.'

'But…' Georgia yelped.

Enrico turned to the embassy staff. 'I think we need to let these two rest. I'll take them to the hotel.'

Enrico helped Georgia into the front seat for the drive.

At the hotel, Brian was surprised by Anne who swamped him with kiss-hungry lips of welcome.

'That's his fiancé,' said Enrico. As he walked Georgia to her room, he advised her. 'Don't mention the money.'

'Money?' asked Georgia.

'Yes, the pouch the man gave you.'

'Oh.'

'I will be flying back with you. I told your brother and his wife that I would see them again, with or without you. They are snakes, sorry to say. Do you have somewhere to stay, or should I organise a hotel?'

'There's my mother's place. It has been rented for years. She left it to me, but I've shared the rent with Paul. Seemed like the right thing. Um.'

'It clearly didn't seem like the right thing to your mother if she left it to you. It's my guess that your brother has moved the tenants out and taken over there too.'

'But, Mum's furniture. Her things. Oh.'

Georgia was granted occupancy of her mother's house, negotiated by a lawyer, who had managed to inform her brother and his wife of their imminent consequences if they delayed or refused.

Georgia lived in a numb haze until a documentary cracked opened her dull heart and released a floodgate of pain. Such a simple thing. A few moments of images flashing on a screen. The Stasi, the Berlin Wall, the fakir beds. But it was neither the stern-faced, uniformed men, nor the concrete structure with its barbed wire defences that brought her down. It was the jubilation, the embraces—the culmination of three decades of weary hopes and dreams.

She slumped against the sliding glass doors. Tears came

then, overdue, like a river whose banks could no longer hold. Looking outside, her eyes sought familiarity, but every inch of the carefully crafted backyard oasis suddenly seemed foreign. The world had tilted. With her forehead on the huge pane, Georgia's ragged breathing fogged the glass. Then, with eyes closed in defeat, she slid to the floor and lay on the cool tiles.

Her mind whirred over the past few days. Georgia experienced a physical ache so deep and profound she feared it would define the rest of her days.

She felt like one of the East Germans who had yearned for the crossing of the forbidden divide, breathed and prayed each day for connection, but then, when the gates were opened there had been no one there. "Family" had evaporated. Her beloved brother had betrayed her. The closeness of their childhood and teen years was gone, or had it ever been what she thought/

Something inside broke away and with each rush of tears, the pain eased. Curved against the door, she smeared the fog left by her breath. With eyes wide open Georgia dared to look outside again. She saw the tips of the camellia leaves where the harsh sun had burned them, the pile of leaves swept up after the storm but not picked up. And further, in the light of the full moon images of the neighbouring houses peaked through the shrubbery.

It was home, and it was hers.

Silently gliding the door open, Georgia padded out on to the patio. A light fall of rain tapped gently on the patio roof. Leaning into the hard brick wall she revelled in its solidness.

The 'too-woot' of an owl punctuated the still night air. She could see the silhouette of Melanie, the dance instructor, in the window of the house that backed onto hers, as she did her evening stretches. She was later than usual, it was nearing midnight. The cat flap clattered next door as the neighbour Frank's cat, Cookie, returned home. She heard the rumble of Frank's low voice as he scolded the cat for 'being out carousing'. Now he could seal the cat flap for the night and turn out the light. The rituals of safety.

It had been so important to grow a privacy barrier between herself and her neighbours. But tonight, she relished their unknowing company.

Gradually the steady beat of her heart and the rhythm of her breathing soothed her. She was home. She was safe.

Thunder cracked and seemed to shake the earth and every building and creature on it. The wind picked up speed and the rain fell in a torrent. She moved quickly to return inside, then stopped. Instead, she sat on the porch swing. She'd never sat through a storm. Dylan found them terrifying and she'd spent every storm comforting him. But now, while Dylan slept deeply with a purring Zeke tucked under his chin, there was no one to comfort. Pushing aside the nagging thought that she was without comfort Georgia allowed herself to be caught up in the majesty of nature's dramatic symphony. It was only a storm. It was outside of her.

Days had passed since the confrontation with her brother. A lifetime had slipped away. The breach seemed impossible, unthinkable. Family ... was it gone forever? She thought of Dylan sleeping inside. No, family was here. 'Family' had to be redefined. Frank and Eileen, with their concern and care were family. Melanie and her three girls, with their afternoon visits through the break in the hedge—were family.

Georgia walked through the house, no longer trembling; the pins and needles in her hands had vanished. Her stomach growled. She'd eaten nothing but apples and muesli bars for days. After heating and devouring a microwave meal, her ravenous appetite sated, she sat at her mother's writing desk. Lovingly tracing a finger over its ridges, she rolled the top back. It hadn't been opened for years, since her mother died. She had hastily thrown things in the drawers. It was a shame not to use such a beautiful piece of furniture. However, until now, it hadn't felt like hers.

Throwing back the thick drapes, she allowed the moonlight to invade the room with dim light. She should rest, but she was wide awake. This desk deserved to be used, this room deserved light and air. Climbing onto the chair she flicked the heavy curtains from the tracks, watching with satisfaction as they fell to the floor. A smile curved her lips.

Venturing into the half-light of the kitchen she found the furniture polish and carrying several cleaning rags she returned and sat in the chair. It was comfortable, familiar.

Impatient with the wonder of claiming the past she placed the polish and rags on the floor, and began opening drawers.

The first thing she saw was the stained, crumbled roll of rupaya that she had stowed there on her return from Pakistan. They were just as they had been when Moussad placed them in her hand. Slipping the rubber band from the notes she flattened them on the desk as she drifted back in time.

She remembered the sinking dread that she could be facing the last day of her life when she had been summoned by the tall stranger with the deep rumbling voice. The man, Moussad, had spoken of family then too. How strange it was to feel at peace with that memory, when all her senses had been screaming as the old woman pulled back the curtain separating the kitchen from the front room in the old house that had been her prison.

The notes were a brilliant purple. Why had she kept them? Was it because of their beauty? Or because of the reversal of grace given her that day? It didn't matter. She would always keep them. Turning one note over, she touched the Urdu wording with reverence, marvelling at the elegance of the script

حصولرزقحلاللعبادتہے

Georgia couldn't remember the pronunciation, but she would never forget the cadence in Moussad's voice as he had read it to her, and translated the words of the prophet Hadith, 'Seeking honest livelihood is worship of God.'

Moussad was a man of substance and spirit, who had returned to his home in the backblocks of Abbottabad to undo the rash acts of his younger brother and nephews. Family. Instead of accepting the ransom money, Moussad had given them both a thick roll of rupaya, each one 50 Rs, along with his sincere regrets.

Georgia replaced the notes in the rubber band. She had vowed never to part with the money, or the story. She hadn't even counted the notes. Their value was not easily reckoned. Returning them to the drawer she remembered Moussad had called her 'the woman without voice'.

The events of the last months had brought the many silences of her life to the surface. How long could she remain 'the woman without voice'?

Moussad was not the only man to treat her with kindness. Brian's brother Enrico had been silently working in the background, championing her fight for justice, for the return of the funds taken. Enrico. He would be there in a few days.

Her hands began to tremble. Gripping the desk, she pushed herself upright and strode into the bedroom to retrieve her laptop. She set it up on her newly claimed work area with determined movements and waited for the screen to flicker to life. She googled the Berlin Wall. Maybe she would find strength, hope there. Something. Anything.

An image filled the screen; as different as night from day to the images that had been the catalyst for her tears. The photograph had been taken from West Berlin, the other side of the wall. Vibrant with colour, it was a montage of art. Selecting it as 'screensaver' she turned the computer off. Every time she used her laptop it would remind her of what was possible on the other side of captivity. The other side of silence.

Enrico arrived early surprising her. He carried so many bright flowers that she hadn't seen him, thought he was a deliver man.

'It's you,' she said breathlessly.

'Very eloquent, Georgia Stone! Who did you think it was? Are you so accustomed to receiving truckloads of flowers that you didn't expect me?'

Georgia hiccupped, smiled widely and opened the door. All the wonderful hours with him on the phone came back in a flood.

Enrico stood inside the door while Georgia fussed over finding a vase.

Their backs touched. They turned.

With but a heartbeat later and an inch to breach, they were kissing. Neither of them had expected this, but neither was surprised. It was the most natural thing in the world.

His lips were full and supple, gently tasting her sweetness.

It was unlike any other kiss Georgia had known. He was giving, not taking; leaving her to set the pace. Putting her in complete control, deliberately taking his time. This released a freedom in Georgia that gave her a new kind of safety.

Kissing Dan had always seemed like a collision, a precursor to something else, but with Enrico, the kiss was the destination. He was savouring, creating, nurturing.

Sliding her arms up his chest and linking her hands behind his head, Georgia surrendered completely. This was no grab in the dark, no push or pull. No demand or expectation. It was a moment of sharing.

As they kissed, they talked. As their tongues met and meshed, plunging the sweetness of the other, their words connected their souls.

'My God, you smell wonderful,' said Georgia.

Enrico covered her mouth, deepening the kiss, then retreating to gentle gliding across her lips. Stronger, softer. Yin and Yang.

'How has someone as sweet as you been so long alone?' he

whispered.

Georgia wondered how they were able to speak without the kiss ending, the connection unbroken. 'I'm hiding,' she said, wondering how the truth had escaped her lips when it hadn't even been recognised by her mind.

His tongue sought her again. 'You shouldn't.'

His arms were wrapped around her, neither drawing her closer, nor releasing her. His hands were linked behind the small of her back. They did not wander or roam. There was no hurry. This was passion of a different kind.

'I have wanted this for so long,' he said.

Georgia slid her tongue along the length of his bottom lip, wondering at her audacity. Security - that was it, the word to describe the feeling. Delighting in the moment she rejoiced that passion had words, and not just mindless lust. She could control this, it was okay. It was just a kiss. Okay, lots of kisses that seemed like one long kiss.

'Are you okay?' he asked.

'Oh, okay doesn't begin to describe it,' she said, her mouth never leaving his.

'I shouldn't.'

'You should,' she said.

'Where have you been, where has your soul been before me?' he asked.

'I don't know.'

The warmth of his body was seeping right through her, and still there was no urgency. Continuing his worship of her mouth, Enrico caressed her back. Then, deepening the kiss he held her tighter.

Georgia was no innocent, but still she thought this was just a moment. It would not sear he heart. She would savour, then forget.

Minutes passed.

The world retreated. There was no other sound but their soft words and the melding of the succulence of their lips, gently claiming each other.

'You are really good at this aren't you,' he said.

'Mmm.'

'Is your heart still beating?'

'Hmm? I'm not dead,' she laughed.

'So you're alive.'

'Deliciously.' She sighed.

Without being aware of it, Georgia's response was increasing. And yet Enrico didn't advance or retreat. Feeling safer, she touched his face, the stubble and the smooth. Manly. She revelled in the joy of being in the arms of a man. This man. Barely aware in a hidden corner of her mind that this man was the only one who could move her this way. Gently, exquisitely.

She could not contemplate the kiss ending, but neither could she imagine passion intruding. Until he took both his hands and, gently touching her neck he moved them slowly through her hair. Sucking in a ragged breath, she moved her arms to embrace his chest.

Her breathing was uneven now and with a flash she knew she was undone.

Enrico's breathing changed too, it was deeper, hungrier. 'You are too lovely...' he murmured, his voice altered. he gathered her closer.

It was then she knew he was undone too. This was so much more than a kiss.

'How can my lips ever leave yours?' he rasped gently.

Her arms tightened around him. 'They shouldn't.'

The mobile in his pocket rang. Drawing away from her, Enrico flipped it open.

'No Brian, I haven't found your bloody laptop.'

Georgia felt bereft, yearning.

The longing in his eyes warmed her. He trailed a finger down her arm. 'I have to go,' he said, 'but don't leave the place we've been. Don't hide, not from me.'

'You'll be … ?'

'I'll be back.'

I Want to Go Home Now

'At exactly what time did you find the victim?' asked Detective George James. His voice was calm and precise—almost indifferent, but Amanda did not miss the sharp intensity in his eyes. She sighed extravagantly.

'Precisely how many times are you going to ask me the same question?' she countered, fanning herself with the official statement forms that had been placed in front of her over an hour ago.

'It's police procedure Miss Sleight, you know that,' he said, quelling a desire to grind his teeth.

'You presume too much, George,' said Amanda. 'How on earth would I know anything of police procedure?—being, as you so clearly pointed out to the Sergeant, I'm 'nothing but a gossipy florist.' She pinned him with clear blue eyes. If the paper she was using as a fan created an unwelcome breeze in his face, Detective James did not show it.

She was deliberately ruffling his feathers, but she didn't care. She saw his jaw tense and almost felt sorry for him. She had found Harry Campbell dead inside her florist shop at opening time, then consoled the man's distraught widow. All the while, trying to hide a large overdue account run up by that woman's unfaithful husband for extravagant floral arrangements for other women. An account which the poor delicate thing would never see.

After all that, and the ensuing questions, Amanda Sleight was well and truly sick of the sight of pompous Det. George James. She knew it was grossly inappropriate to use his first name, but if she hadn't overheard his disdainful remarks to the duty Sergeant, she would not have been goaded beyond endurance.

Detective George James loosened his tie, perhaps indicating that this was going to take a while.

'Amanda, you don't have to make this harder than it already is. I'm sorry for what I said. I was out of line. You're not gossipy, you're just friendly. Please accept my apology.'

He smiled. Amanda ceased her fanning movements just long enough to give him a sharp look of disgust. Det. James began again, his voice tight.

'I'm know you watch enough late-night crime shows to realise that I'm only doing my job,' he said.

The fact that he knew her evening occupations only pushed Amanda further towards the brink of losing her temper completely. The only reason he knew about her life was because they had shared those evenings with an intimacy that died as quickly as Harry Campbell, the victim. Amanda snapped the papers onto the desk.

'That's low, George!' she said, barely controlling the pain in her voice. 'Bringing our private times into the conversation.'

'Well, it's common knowledge that the very married Harry Campbell spent a lot of time in your presence.'

A tense silence followed, while Amanda pursued her tired thoughts. She saw the past months and George's changing demeanour in a new light. Her mind began to race. So that was it. The wretch! How could he think it of her? Fury gnawed at her stomach. She slipped into icy calm.

'Scumbag cheating husbands with many 'interests' tend to find themselves in frequent need of expensive floral arrangements.' She paused. 'Let's see - there's the "understated thank you" arrangement, the "shy enticement bouquet", the "initial seduction arrangement" ... oh, and—the rushed after-hours visit to my home to order the "guilty extravaganza for the suspicious wife."

She let the that sink in, watching George's Adam's apple dance in his throat. Then she saw enlightenment in his eyes.

Picking up her handbag, and pushing the papers towards George, she stood.

'I will answer no more questions. I did not kill Harry Campbell. I am, however, experiencing a strong desire to kill *you*, George James. Put that in your stinking report. I want to go home now.'

Amanda Sleight smoothed her short charcoal skirt, retrieved her red clutch, and left. She would have been most gratified to see Det. George James banging his head on the desk, if only she'd turned to look. But she had walked briskly down the corridor, her footsteps echoing.

George James silently flicked through his Teledex. Where on earth would he find another florist as good as Amanda? He could hardly make arrangements for an "apology bouquet" from Amanda's store.

Never too late for a hero

Wesley stood outside the office of Goodwin Investigations & Recovery Agency. It was an old stone building in an upmarket area of the city. He was early for an interview as personal assistant. The Goodwin Agency was prestigious. The hours were flexible and the pay rate was more than generous. He loved being an artist, but even though his paintings sold well, the money was irregular.

Taking a moment to check his appearance in the large glass windows, he realised he should have had a haircut. He put a hand up to tidy his hair and saw a daub of paint on his hand. So much for a good first impression.

While the Estefan's Café & Restaurant opposite was enjoying brisk trade, there was no-one on the Agency side of the street. Wesley wondered how many other applicants would be attending. Squaring his shoulders, he pushed open the ancient timber and glass door. A bell tinkled in the back room. He looked around. The office resembled something out of the Forties with its antique furniture.

A tall elegant woman was shuffling papers on a mahogany desk that dominated the room. 'Drat,' she said, as a sheaf of papers hit the ground and slid across the floor.

Wesley stooped to retrieve them.

'Don't worry, young man. I'll do it later. I need to pick them up in a particular order.' The woman tucked a stray strand of coal black hair into an off-kilter bun that was held in place with a pencil. 'I'm Veronica Goodwin, owner, investigator, dogsbody, you name it. And you are Wesley Brent.' She twisted around, eyes scanning the room. 'Now where are those … darn, can't find a thing. Nice to meet you.' With a wide smile she reached out and shook his hand. 'Well, Wesley Brent, you can see my drastic need for a personal assistant.' She gestured at the shambles of paperwork on her desk. 'Please take a seat.'

Wesley folded his lanky frame onto the chair. He opened his mouth to begin the spiel he'd been rehearsing for days, but Veronica had flipped open the laptop computer and was tapping random keys.

'Wretched thing. I hope you understand it,' she said. The computer beeped into life. Veronica squeaked in surprise. She shuffled the papers on her desk. 'Oh there they are,' she said, placing a dark rimmed pair of glasses on her face with a satisfied sigh. 'I hope you'll like it here, Wesley. The job is yours.'

'Oh? I thought this was an interview. The employment agency told me to bring these.' Wesley held up a black folder.

'Daft lot, those agency people. I have all your information on file.'

Wesley's eyebrows flew up. 'You do?'

'Naturally. Um, cyberspace, internet, you know.' She pointed at the computer, eyeing it suspiciously.

'Ah, the agency sent my information. Of course.'

Veronica frowned, then seemed relieved. 'Ah yes, that must be it.' The computer pinged. Veronica shut the lid down. 'I see you're quite the artist.'

'How did you know that?' Wesley squirmed in the chair.

'I've seen you painting the mural for the Estefans café opposite.'

'Oh, of course.'

Veronica leaned back. 'I believe you are perfect for the job Wesley. You have a good reputation for confidentiality.'

'But I haven't worked as a personal assistant before.'

'You're much too humble Wesley Brent. Always have been. Why that fiasco back at University, with the student newspaper—you only wanted to protect Sara, of course, sorting the petty cash theft by replacing the money yourself. Wouldn't have worked the second time though.'

'Say again.' Wesley sat bolt upright. 'How can you possibly know any of this? *Were you there*? This is bizarre.' Wesley mopped his forehead with a handkerchief that had seen better days.

'Oh Wesley, the world is never quite what it seems.' Veronica smiled. 'I'll start from the beginning…'

Wesley slumped in the chair. Veronica brought him a glass of water.

'I'm a time traveller Wesley, you know—travelling to different…' Wesley choked on the sip of water. When the coughing fit ceased, he viewed the woman opposite him with watery eyes and a shocked expression.

'Oh dear. You look like you want to run out the door. Please stay and hear me out, Wesley.'

'Don't think I could stand if I tried.'

'I'll give you time to take it all in. I can almost see the cogs in your head turning. You were like that back then too.'

'So you *were* there. I don't remember seeing you. Were you invisible?'

Veronica laughed. 'One Superpower at a time please!'

'Wait a minute—you said something about the *second* time. There wasn't a second theft.'

'Ah Wesley, but there so very nearly was.'

Wesley leaned forward, alert. 'Ah. I know. A week after the money went missing I was working late on the artwork for the paper. There was an almighty noise, but there was nothing out of place. I would've searched longer but Sara phoned me from the hospital. Her father had broken his leg.'

Regret flashed across Veronica's face. 'Were you alone in the building, Wesley?'

'Well yes. Everyone had gone home. Wait on, there was just a janitor, some new woman. Said she hadn't seen anything, kept her head down. Funny sort of a…Oh my god, *that was you!*'

Veronica nodded. 'There was a reason you were protecting Sara. Apart from the massive crush you had on her. You thought she knew something.'

Wesley flushed.

'Oh, you poor dear. You're still carrying a flame for the girl. After ten years. It was a noble thing to do—replacing the money. Ill advised, but noble.'

'Sara was the only other one with the keys to the office. But I knew it wasn't her.'

'And you were right. She didn't. It was her father.'

Wesley's face turned white. 'Her father? *Bill took it!*'

The phone jangled. Veronica picked it up, and in perfect diction spoke into the mouthpiece. 'You have reached the office of Goodwin Investigations & Recovery Agency. This is an automated message. We apologise for not being available, but your call is important to us. Please leave a message and we will return your call.'

Wesley's mouth dropped open. 'You're very good, you think quickly. Guess you've been doing it for centuries.' He held up a hand. 'Don't tell me. I don't want to know. But, how did Bill take the money?'

'Simple really. Crime often is. He only had to stay hidden in the staff toilets in the main administration block at closing time, then slip out the fire exit afterwards. Security wasn't great in those days, as you'll remember. He was disappointed to find less than $50 the first time so he decided to make another attempt.'

'Oh dear, this is starting to make sense. Bill was always short of cash. He would borrow from Sara. I'm pretty sure he had a gambling problem. But I never thought he'd do something like that. Sara can't possibly know. It would break her heart.' Wesley ran tense fingers through his hair. 'I was just returning from the toilets when I heard the ruckus. What on earth did you do to stop him?'

'Simple. I came rattling past with the cleaning trolley. Bill got a shock, lost his balance, then ran off.'

'But his broken leg?' Wesley rested his elbows on the desk,

watching Veronica intently.

'Bill's, er, shall we say *loan officer*, was waiting for the money in the car park with a couple of thugs.'

'Bill claimed he'd stopped to help a homeless man and been attacked. My God, the lies he told.'

'Bill was trouble. I think that's why Sara has that bad boy attraction thing going on. It's often the way, it's why nice guys like you finish last.'

'Just for once I'd like to finish first, with Sara. Do you think…?'

A loud knock at the door deferred any words of wisdom Veronica may have offered. It was Estella Estefan with two pizza boxes. The aroma filled the room. Wesley's stomach growled.

'Estella, how kind,' said Wesley, ushering the woman inside with a grin, 'but where is Veronica's pizza? She'll be hungry too.'

Estella slapped his arm. 'You tease an old woman too much, Wesley. One is for your new boss. You have the job? Yes?'

Veronica nodded and laughed.

'Good,' said Estella. 'Don't you be letting this one have your pizza, Senora. Like a horse he eats and yet he stays thin and handsome. It's enough to make a woman cry.'

After they had eaten, Veronica became crisp and businesslike, filling Wesley in on his duties. She swept around the room, filling the air with exotic perfume as she detailed his role and explained the filing system and client records.

Wesley's eyes widened when Veronica told him that her previous assistant, Evan, was still back in time. 'He's lost, somewhere,' she said, quickly wiping a tear aside. 'So you see, you really must be very particular.'

Veronica handed Wesley a handwritten list.

Stay close.

Follow instructions immediately without question.

Don't act on any other matter except the case in hand.

Don't interact with anyone you know unless it's unavoidable.

If you speak to anyone, say nothing to affect their destiny.

Worry lines creased Wesley's forehead as he contemplated the last line. He held it up. 'I hope you don't expect me to eat this Veronica, because I don't think I could fit it in after all that pizza.'

'You've been watching too many movies.' Veronica laughed. 'And they said you were boring.'

'Who said that?' Wesley shrugged. 'Never mind, I don't want to know.'

'Precisely why I hired you, Wesley Brent. Tomorrow we begin…'

As soon as Wesley walked through the door the next morning he saw Veronica buzzing around the room. She retrieved a small card from the file with a photograph attached.

'This one will do today, Wesley.' She tapped the client card with a red nailed finger. 'Are you ready?'

The first mission wasn't what he had anticipated. He'd expected to be involved in preventing some terrible event in history—a bombing or a plane crash at the very least. But that first assignment had been a tense waiting game in a seedy downtown bar, late on a wintry night a mere ten years in the past.

A middle aged socialite had paid an exorbitant fee for Veronica to intercept her husband, an ageing Don Juan, from meeting his current mistress. Because the wife had no way of knowing the exact moment her husband had met the dazzling creature who'd become his latest lover, Veronica and Wesley endured a long wait.

The prospective mistress was in an upstairs room singing a collection of sultry ballads. The cheating husband didn't arrive for hours. Finally, he swept through the door bringing an icy blast.

Veronica flicked a cigarette lighter near the fire sensor. A narrow flame rose and flickered unnoticed. The alarm shrieked. Chaos reigned. Patrons screamed and shoved, desperate to escape. Wesley seized the man's arm and ushered him into a waiting taxi. The would-be lover was on his way in a matter of minutes, none the wiser.

Over the next few months Veronica relaxed. Wesley was sure she had grown to trust him. She didn't comment any further about Evan. Perhaps he had failed to stay near her when they were on a mission or broken one of the other rules.

They slipped into an easy routine. Veronica gave him a brief outline of the mission ahead along with concise instructions. Then they entered the creaky lift at the rear of the building; their conduit to another time. Veronica used an ornate fob watch to select the parameters of their destination. When they stepped out of the lift they were at the precise location and time she'd programmed.

It was Wesley's job to arrange incidentals. Detours and meals were often necessary and it was also his role to source the correct money and maps. Wesley hadn't imagined these necessities, but it made sense that even supernatural powers needed organisation. Once they were on assignment, Veronica had bigger things to worry about.

When the mission was accomplished, Veronicawould signal to Wesley. Taking the small black mobile he'd been given, he pressed#. That summoned the lumbering George with their taxi. The taxi was different according to the era, but it was always George who collected them. When they were in the taxi Veronica tapped the watch. They were instantly back in the lift at the office.

To Wesley's disappointment, the assignments continued to be mundane. They stopped Mrs Damson's Labrador wandering from home. They travelled back to the day Mrs Wiltshire decided to dye her hair a fiery red. One assignment had involved showing up at a ritzy hotel to remind a young bride-to-be to pick up her handbag containing a ridiculously expensive engagement ring.

They sent Mrs Beverly home early from the supermarket the day the decorators were due, forestalling a 'truly hideous colour choice' by her husband who was taking revenge on his wife for inviting her mother to stay.

Wesley consoled himself with the thought that his new life was the closest he'd ever come to being a hero. Anyway, he had plenty to keep him busy. There was research in the library building to ascertain whether the client was attempting to use their services for criminal purposes. 'Better safe than sorry,' Veronica said. And there was always the weather to check.

Winter slipped into spring. Wesley finished painting the mural for the Estefans and had arranged to meet Sara at the café after work. The mural was a vibrant portrayal of life in Italy. Wesley had painted all the Estefan family members from their village, sitting at tables and dancing in the square.

The last rays of the sun slanted onto the rooftops. Wesley whistled as he walked. He was looking forward to spending the evening with Sara. The café was their favourite eatery. It was full of the aromas of Italy and throbbed with the hum of friendship and life. Inside, the stucco walls were painted a muted crimson. The floor was covered with black and white harlequin tiles that shone and sparkled all day. Estella achieved this by rolling out the ancient metal bucket and mop at least half a dozen times a day.

Wesley greeted them and sat with Dimitri.

'Oi, that woman, she makes me tired,' Dimitri said. 'She will wash away the tiles and we will have just concrete left.'

Estella swished the mop in the direction of her husband. 'Why are you sitting old man?' she asked. The men exchanged sly looks and grinned. 'Oh, you have finish our mural Wesley? May I see? Dimitri does not let me have even one peek.'

'Come woman, and stop your bellyaching at me.' Dimitri led the way outside.

Estella wiped her apron across watery eyes. 'Bellissimo Wesley! Where did you learn such things? It is just like home.' Her voice was rich and caressing. She embraced Wesley. 'Why did you not wait for Sara? Oh see, here she is now.'

Wesley turned. Sara had left her corporate image behind. Her long chestnut hair was loose and she wore a casual sundress. She looked like sunshine, young and free. The image of her in the twilight reminded him of the first time he'd seen her at their University orientation event. He found it hard to breathe and hoped she didn't notice.

Estella bounded up to meet Sara and swept her aside. 'Ciao bella. Is not the mural Wesley painted bellisimo? He is wonderful. And so are you, coming to help an old man with his accounts. Grazie, molte grazie.'

Estella cleared the tables while Wesley swept the floor.

Dimitri sat at the corner table with Sara. He leant over the old ledger stained with sauces from the kitchen. The old man watched the earnest young woman tally the accounts; her eyes alight with enthusiasm.

'How can you love numbers on a page?' Dimitri said, 'when there is so much more.' He placed his hand on his heart.

Sara looked up. 'Are you all right, Dimitri?'

'Of course, cara. It is *your* heart I think about. It is for you time to fall in love.'

Sara laughed. 'I have had too much love, Dimitri.'

'You have had too much something, I think. But it is not too much love.'

'I keep getting love wrong, Dimitri.'

'It's not the love you get wrong cara, I think you maybe get the wrong man.' Dimitri removed his glasses and wiped them on his red handkerchief. 'Don't listen to me. I'm just an old man who wishes everyone happy.' He glanced across at Wesley who was emptying bins while Estella sang to the pigeons crooning on the beams under the awnings. 'Come, enough work. Wesley, join us and celebrate.'

Dimitri brought two bottles of red wine, dragging Estella from her cleaning on the way.

As the chill of the evening fell, Estella lit the candles and coaxed Dimitri to dance with her.

Wesley took Sara's hands and led her to a space between the tables. He pulled her close. 'This will have to be a very slow dance Sara, there's not much room.'

'The mural is wonderful, Wesley,' said Sara. 'I don't know how you've had time for it. You've been helping me set up my new office on top of your own work. It's a big step for me, starting an accountancy practice on my own. I couldn't have done it without you, you know. You're my best friend.' She gave a nervous laugh. 'I don't know how you've put up with me. All those tears I've cried on your shoulder over some stupid man.'

Wesley struggled to find words, but couldn't. Instead, he kissed the top of her head. Just one tear for me, Sara. I'd give anything for you to cry one tear for me, he thought.

Sara put down her glass and took Wesley's hand. 'I have something I want to ask you.'

Wesley's eyes searched hers.

'I would really like you to be my partner in the business. We're a great team.'

Disappointment formed a lump in Wesley's throat. 'I'm sorry, Sara. I have a job,' he said, his voice thin. 'It's, well it's important. I help Veronica find things and people, make a difference.' He spun her around, forcing a smile and cursing his cowardice for not revealing the real reason—that it would be unbearable to see her all the time, loving her as he did. Friendship would have to do.

'I'm sorry. I shouldn't have asked,' she said.

He blanched at the pain in her eyes. He smiled to soften the words. They continued to dance, but the mood between them had changed. Estella chided the grandchildren for peeking when they should have been in bed. Wesley heard the deep rumble of Dimitri's words of love to his wife and her laughing response. He experienced a sharp pang of longing and drew Sara closer.

The next morning Wesley woke early and ran a hasty hand through his hair. His mind was annoyingly foggy. He must have had too much red wine. While Sara was in his arms he had almost hoped … but now he had to focus on the day and the next mission. When he arrived at the office Veronica briefed him. Derby Day, Kentucky, 1974. A father had gambled away his daughter's college fund on a 20-1 horse named Patience.

At the races they recognised their target from the photo his daughter had provided. The man was waiting for the betting booth to open. He paced, patting a fat wallet. Veronica tipped a glass of wine on him and began a long-winded argument with him. He missed the queue.

'That's great,' said Wesley. 'All over quickly.'

'I wish it was that simple. There are three more days of the racing carnival.'

'Oh. He's still going to blow his money, isn't he?'

Veronica sighed. 'If he gets the chance. We'll have to stay. Tramping around a soggy racetrack isn't my idea of fun but we have to see this through.'

Wesley wondered if Veronica ever tired of time travel. Being a Superhero wasn't all it was cracked up to be as far as he could see. He booked them into a small Bed & Breakfast near the racecourse.

Their man was a vain and superficial creature who seemed to care only for fancy clothes, inane conversation and copious quantities of whisky, and survived on a few hours' sleep at night. Wesley could quietly murder him. God only knows what *that* would do to the cosmos. Veronica was in fine form. She managed to prevent the man from placing a single bet. After the final race was run, the two time travellers sat exhausted in the refreshments marquee.

'The last three days have been the most terminally boring of my entire life,' said Wesley, resting his head on the back of the chair.

Veronica dropped her wine glass.

Wesley touched her arm. 'Veronica! You're as white as a ghost!'

Veronica's hands shook. Her eyes were fixed on some point in the straggling crowd that was streaming towards the exit gates. All at once she was off, throwing herself into the jubilant arms of a well-built man with a thatch of blonde hair. Spinning her around, the man rained kisses on her neck.

Wesley froze.

'What the…? Veronica! You'll mess with the time space

continuum thingy.'

Veronica turned to face him, her arm firmly around the man beside her. 'It's all right, Wesley.'

'No it's not! This can't be good, it's dangerous. It's against the rules—*your* rules.' He reached for his notebook. It wasn't in his pocket. 'This can't be happening. We'll never get home.'

'Wesley, stop. This is … my assistant, the one I lost, remember?'

Wesley gaped at them. 'Evan?'

'Yes, Evan. Evan *Goodwin*.' Veronica placed a gloved hand on Wesley's arm. 'Everything is as it should be, Wesley.' She peeled the glove from her hand, revealing a wedding ring. 'This is where I belong. Here with Evan; in the past.'

'Oh! I see,' he said, scratching his head.' Actually, I don't see at all.'

Veronica smiled a soft smile of regret. 'Think about it, dear man.'

'Oh, my! So, I'm from the future.'

'Yes, Wesley dear.'

It was quiet in the taxi with George. Wesley watched the outside world blur by the darkened taxi window.

'What happens now, George?'

'Whatever you choose, Wesley.' George handed him the fob watch; the key to going home.

Wesley looked down at the watch. The legacy of time travel was now his to accept or reject. He could be the next Superhero if he wished.

Wesley handed the watch back. 'You tap it George. I'm

going home. For Good.'

He ran from the lift. The office didn't even warrant a sideways glance. He needed Sara, wanted her. He would accept the partnership. She might come to love him. It was worth the chance.

Sara stared out into the darkness. The city lights blinked mutely. Where on earth was Wesley? He'd been gone for days. She wound her hair around tense fingers, wavering between anxiety about his safety and anger that he hadn't called. Now and then, she wiped salty wetness from her face.

She thought of everything they'd been through together. All the times he had been her calm and stable rock. She thought of the weeks she had spent with him after his parents died, when he hadn't been able to face the world. She'd made him get up and keep going, forced him to eat, gone through every corner of the cottage he grew up in, sorting all the possessions of his parents' lives. She remembered all the times they'd helped each other shift. When had her feelings turned to love? How had she ever been content with friendship with this wonderful man? The one who never let her down. She wept bitter tears. Tears for Wesley.

Finally, as the pink dust of dawn intruded she curled into a ball on the sofa and fell asleep.

There was a loud rap on the door.

She flung it open.

'Sara, you really must remember to check who's at the door before you … Oh no, you've been crying.'

She crushed him to her.

'Who hurt you this time?' Wesley murmured against her ear. 'I'll kill him.'

'Then you will have to kill yourself, you idiot! Where have you been? I've been worried out of my mind!' She rained salty kisses on him.

'I haven't been gone that long,' he said. 'What do you mean? I'm the one who hurt you?'

'Do I have to spell it out for you Wesley?' Sara's eyes sparkled.

'Yes, please.' Wesley drew her closer and manoeuvred them to the couch where he pulled her into his lap. 'Spelling would be great. I've always liked spelling. Did I tell you I once won a spell…'

Sara silenced him with a lingering kiss.

'I think you misspelled that. You may have to do it again.'

Sara laughed. 'I love you.'

'It's about time. I've loved you for ages.' Wesley smiled. 'Now *do* stop interrupting a perfectly good spelling lesson.' He returned her kisses with all the passion of those hungry years.

Blue eyes

Oh dear God! 'Be still my beating heart', thought Kayla as she gunned her Ute out of the car park, spewing gravel and barely missing a pedestrian. The man was gorgeous.

Of course it was her luck to see him in the middle of a frantic early morning dash to the local hardware store. It also had to be on a day when she had tied a cleaning rag around her hair. Tearing out of the door she had thrown a faded denim shirt over a lacy singlet top.

'*Kayla*, your underwear is showing!' her shocked mother declared.

Underwear my eye. Her mother was such a dinosaur. The strappy top cost a fortune and was a soft grey with fuchsia lace edging. It was a rare celebration of her femininity. Just because she renovated houses didn't mean she had to look like a complete fashion tragic.

On any other day she might have attempted to saunter casually past the gorgeous man and engineer a 'chance' meeting. She could have dropped her keys or exercised some other female ploy that she'd read about. Naturally, she couldn't try any of those tricks because she was driving her car, making all those things completely useless. She could hardly drive back round to the car park after her manic exit and coolly pretend to 'bump' into him. None of the romantic movies or stories of her experience had ever begun by mowing down the object of your desire.

The plastic buckets she had bought to mix her next batch of milk paint leaned perilously towards her from their place in the passenger seat. She was in a complete strop as she roared past him. Their eyes connected. He turned his head to watch her tire-squealing exit. She could have sworn his eyes held a mixture of awe and attraction. But what would she know? It had been a long time since a man had caused such an instant reaction to the pit of her stomach. It was purely physical. She shouldn't have skipped breakfast.

Anyway, it didn't matter. She would never see him again. He didn't look as if he was from around here. It was a small community where everyone knew everyone; at least in a tacit head nodding way. Truth be told, he didn't look as if he was from anywhere she'd ever been. He belonged in Hollywood but he looked a little rugged.

Dark, negligently waving hair contrasted with dreamy blue eyes. She just loved the combination of dark hair and blue eyes. Why *was that*? Was she genetically programmed? He was wearing a chambray blue shirt, a bold manly blue that matched his eyes. One hand was casually thrust into the pocket of chocolate chinos. Oh damn, now she would think of him every time she saw chocolate.

If she hadn't been in such a snarly mood she might have still been strolling the car park casually and walked into him instead of nearly running over him. Mind you, his eyes had lit up and a beautiful smile creased his fabulous face. Perhaps he had a preference for maniacal stroppy women who drove beat up Ute's. It was probably better that she had missed the opportunity for conversation. Her hair was still a disaster from her early morning swim in the pool. She could have tried out her new eye batting techniques but her eyes looked crap without gobs of mascara.

The snarly mood had started yesterday when the timber for the skirting board failed to arrive. This morning things had only gotten worse. Much worse. Her frantic dash to the hardware included not one, but two lengthy stops for road works. She only wanted a strip of muslin to strain the milk paint and two plastic buckets.

'All this for a piece of fabric,' she muttered in frustration. Great, now she was talking to herself.

She could have spit nails when the helpful guy in the paint section said they had no muslin and that he had used his wife's pantyhose to strain paint the last time he made milk paint. This was a trick she remembered, but she had thrown all her pantyhose in the trash when she'd sworn off men. She was glad at the time. Take Jeff. Never mind, nobody needed to take Jeff because he had taken himself off and out of her life. She was well rid of him.

But that was months ago—22 to be exact. Not that she was counting.

In the rear vision mirror she could see the tall man watching her drive off. He was certainly breaking her man drought. She developed a serious thumping of the heart and jelly legs. Just as well she was sitting down. Sadly, she was driving away from the liberator of her lost libido. She moaned out loud.

She momentarily considered driving back and pretending to have forgotten something. She did that often enough lately. If she had made a list before going to the hardware store yesterday she could have saved herself grief today. As it was, she had been there three times yesterday. Honestly, where was her head? She vowed never to get in a strop again. She'd even argued with the television yesterday so she was definitely losing it.

The handsome stranger stirred her. She would have to put herself 'out there' again. All she had to do was discover the mystery location of 'out there'. Never mind. All was not lost; she would make good use of the buzz the gorgeous man brought to life.

However, before she put herself 'out there' she had to go to the supermarket and buy a pair of pantyhose – for the paint. As she turned into the supermarket car park she was stopped by yet another road worker. The Ute was half in and half out of the entrance, blocking the traffic from both directions. She saw a huge pile of sand. No-one would be going in there for a while.

All her intentions of never having a bad mood for the rest of her life went out the window. She reversed quickly back into the stream of the traffic and roared off down the street, leaving early morning shoppers open mouthed in shock.

Then she remembered another option. The craft shop would have muslin. Turning into the parking lot near the shop she sighed and wondered if she would ever see Mr Gorgeous again. Oh dear, I am being very Jane Austen, how desperate. It wasn't likely that he would be in a craft shop. He was too well dressed for a delivery man and he would hardly be buying a few yards of fabric to whip up another stunning blue shirt to match his 'get lost in the ocean' eyes.

The fantasy died quickly. The only other shop in that whole street was the Op Shop. He was too up-market for there either. He was too tanned and virile to be doing good works inside a dusty charity shop.

He looked more like a sales rep. She laughed out loud as she thought of the improbability of a sales rep of any kind going to the Op Shop—'Would you care to see our latest line of second-hand tea towels, Madam?' As if! Her mood lifted.

The craft shop was mercifully quiet and she chatted with Georgina, the elderly owner who also ran the quilting classes. Georgina gave her one metre of muslin free of charge as Kayla was contracted to paint the store. She had already rendered the brick walls and would start painting in earnest the following week. Jauntily stepping out of the craft shop, she looked down to avoid the dodgy top step that usually had a gaggle of old ladies gathered around it moaning about its potential for causing an accident.

She walked straight into Mr Gorgeous and looked into the blue of the Mediterranean ocean and every other ocean of her dreams. His eyes were even more incredible up close. He was holding her with both arms to steady her. Which she very much needed now that she was so near him. But not because of the dodgy step.

Her usual motor mouth lost its batteries. She was gawping like a guppy.

'You have quite a driving style,' he said with a cheeky grin that was reflected in the ocean eyes. So he remembered her; interesting.

'Yes, I was Peter Brock in a past life,' she riposted.

Damn, was that the best she could do?

'You look a bit old for Peter Brock's reincarnation; didn't he 'pass over' not long ago? I may be a sceptic but that seems a very dubious claim.' he said. She was grateful that he was still steadying her with his arms.

'No offense intended,' he added, with another heart stopping smile.

'None taken,' she said generously.

She leaned closer and adopted a conspiratorial whisper. 'There is a new fast track process for reincarnation, 21st Century stuff; Top Secret technology. It's very *hush hush*. So you see, I really *am* Peter Brock.'

'You know, I always wanted to meet Peter Brock.'

This was the perfect time for a flirty response that would overwhelm him with wit and intelligence. Unfortunately, the battery for her mouth died again.

It didn't seem to matter. Her face was an open book; he seemed to be reading everything he wanted to know in her eyes. The smile on his face told her he liked what he was seeing.

'And here you are,' he finished.

Her bones were melting.

'And here I am.'

Lame, lame. She mentally kicked herself.

Amused by her loss of speech but not bothered by it, he let her go gently. He extended a warm brown hand.

'I'm Kieran Stern, by the way.'

She accepted the handshake. The rest of her traitorous body wanted to join in the shaking. Pressing her legs together to support each other, she willed herself to stay upright.

'And I'm Kayla Watkins,' she murmured, 'and I'm not usually a deaf mute.'

'I'll bet you're not,' he roared laughing, 'If your driving is anything to go by!'

A light switched on in her brain. She remembered Georgina talking about her only son who had been helping rebuild housing in Indonesia after the Boxing Day Tsunami. She knew he was returning to live near Georgina after her recent cancer treatment. Kayla had heard so much about him as she sanded and prepared the ancient walls of the craft shop. She had come to know Georgina well.

'Oh, you must be Georgina's son, the one who went overseas to rebuild the orphanage!'

'The very same, although I must say I didn't rebuild the whole orphanage by myself. It's very boring to be thought a saint.' His eyes sparkled.

'I guess it would be,' she responded, 'I haven't had much experience of sainthood but I've heard it can be a real downer.'

He tilted his head to the side and regarded her with humorous eyes. He was enchanted. 'I can believe that,' he said drily.

Kayla tried to frown in mock fury but she had to repress a smile. It was impossible to be offended when the man in front of her was looking at her as if he didn't want to let her go.

'I'm helping my mother refurbish the shop,' he said, still

holding her hand. She was glad they were away from the main street with the inevitable hustle and bustle of the shopping crowds. She repented for every time she had cursed the shop's 'off the beaten track' locale as she lost herself in his eyes.

'Oh really,' she said, trying to dampen her excitement. 'I'm doing the painting.'

'Ah, I was wondering why you had a chisel in your pocket. It's a relief to know that you're not a chisel murderer on the loose.' He was laughing at her.

'I hope you are going to fix that dodgy step,' was all she could muster.

'I'm not sure I should if it delivers beautiful girls into my arms,' he murmured.

She blushed. If this was flirting, she could definitely get used to it.

'So, it looks like we will be working together,' he gently prompted, leaning towards Kayla.

'Looks like.' She couldn't remember a single clever line from any of her trawling of magazine articles. She should have tried harder after the disastrous result when she did the 'Rate Your Flirting Skills' questionnaire in her latest magazine. Apparently a score of two meant you should just give up and join a crochet group.

He handed her down the last of the steps. Her skin tingled and her head began to buzz in an alarming fashion.

'That means I have a little time to get to know you before I pluck up the courage to ask you out.' His smile was totally disarming. The battery to her mouth flickered and died again. She just looked up at him like a mute idiot. He looked down at his hand. Oh dear, she was gripping his hand.

'Or not,' he said, drawing closer. 'We could have a coffee and consolidate our mutual refurbishing plans.' His eyes simmered with hidden meaning.

'I just love a man with a plan,' she said, her eyes bright and teasing. 'I could murder a coffee!'

'If you don't slow down, you'll murder more than a coffee!' he said.

'In that case I will leave my chisel behind. Since you're new in town I know a great little coffee shop,' she said, thinking of the coffee shop attached to the local art gallery. It was even more remote than the craft shop.

'Shall we take my car?' he offered with mock fear in his incredible eyes. 'I'd like to be alive for our next date.'

Over a simple lunch of warm Turkish bread and spicy pumpkin soup they discovered they shared a love of antiques and flea markets. Kayla wondered why she hadn't read in any of the magazines that it was possible to fall in love on a 'bad hair day'.

Kieran found her natural, warm and funny. He discovered it was possible to fall in love with someone who had run out of the house without seeing a great daub of white paint on their cheek.

The first thing Kayla was going to do when she got home was to throw out that flirting test. She didn't need to redo it after all.

Heartbreak Hotel

'I'm going to have to dump her.' Matt Williams pulled a distracted hand through his gleaming hair. He took a step back as his friend Dan brushed past him on the way to the hand basin.

'She's gorgeous,' said Dan Miller, a tense edge to his voice. He had seen his charismatic school friend go through women like a greedy toddler in a toy store. He often wondered why Matt still bothered with him, but as he'd just put in a couple of hours fine-tuning his latest acquisition, a BMW sports car, Dan realised that Matt was using him as much as all his women.

'Yes, she's certainly easy on the eye,' said Matt, looking at Lisa with pride. 'I can sure pull the hotties.'

Dan threw the towel onto the basin, hoping Matt would leave so that he wouldn't have to watch yet another beautiful girl have her heart broken. Usually he didn't care much. The types that hung off Dan were usually empty-headed vain models who couldn't stand to be around the workshop. Why would he care about this one? He thought she seemed different to the others. Ah, but what would he know? Flicking his cleaning rag into his back pocket he made a great show of gathering his tools, hoping Matt would take the hint and leave.

'You can leave the car with me, you know Matt. I have to wait for the part for a few hours yet.'

'I would mate,' said Matt, eyeing his watch. 'But Lisa wanted to wander around the yard for a while.'

Dan turned surprised eyes to Matt.

'She doesn't exactly look dressed for the occasion. I reckon those designer clothes won't last long in this place.'

'Yeah, beats me why she'd want to be here.'

They both looked at Lisa, who seemed to be in another world. With her sunglasses pushed back onto her head, she was standing with eyes closed, blissfully enjoying the sun on her face. To Dan she looked like a goddess. Her caramel hair fell in careless abandon halfway down her back. She opened her eyes, saw them looking and threw them an artless dazzling smile. She turned to open the black bag she'd been carrying.

'Probably getting her make up out of her purse. Better tell her there's no mirror in the 'bathroom facilities',' said Dan, his voice edged with sarcasm.

He didn't want to like this girl. He was sick of Matt parading his conquests around him. Looking down at his grimy overalls Dan realised he didn't stand a chance with any of the women who fawned all over Matt.

'No, she doesn't wear make-up. She could improve herself a bit if she did. Her hair would look great with blonde streaks too. I've given her the hint - tried to push her towards my stylist, but she says she likes her hair 'wild'. Oh no! She's getting her bloody camera out. She'll be ages. Never leaves home without the thing. She could make a fortune as a model, but no, she's into 'art photography'.' Matt's voice took on a bitter edge. 'I'll be stuck here now. Bloody high maintenance women; don't know how I keep finding them.'

'I've got to get back to work, mate,' said Dan, fast losing patience.

He stole another look at Lisa as she took shots of the outside of the garage. This was a change anyway, one of Matt's women more at home behind the camera rather than playing up to it.

'I mean, they want their own way all the time,' continued Matt.

Dan gave in and leaned negligently against the doorway to the workshop. It seemed Matt wanted a moan, and knowing Matt as he did, Dan knew there was no way out. Might as well get it over with and listen to his narcissistic friend blow off steam. They sooner he'd finished, the sooner Dan could get on with things.

'So, you're chucking her because she's high maintenance?' he asked. Not much in the way of conversation but Dan was bored stiff.

Matt turned fiery eyes to Dan. 'No mate,' he began. 'It's much worse than that. She's been holding out on me.'

'Oh, I see, she won't sleep with you?' Dan grinned. This was a turn up for the books. He could seriously enjoy hearing about a woman impervious to Matt's charms.

'Well, no, it's not that. I mean we haven't slept together. Of course she wants to, but she's been busy.'

Dan's imagination was fired. Deliberately showing his poker face he waited for Matt to continue.

'No she's holding out on me about a kid.' Matt looked into

Dan's eyes. 'That's as low as it gets, right mate? Having an ankle biter and acting like a single woman.'

Dan's eyes narrowed. He was the proud uncle to his sister's children. Chelsea was a single mother with three children.

'I was looking around in her handbag and found baby wipes. And there was this photo of some baby with hair the same colour as hers.' Matt waited for Dan's response.

Dan saw Matt look around for a chair and decided to take action. He'd had enough.

'I tell you what mate. I'll get Damien to take you back to the car dealership, so you don't lost a sale on one of your prestige cars. Ms Sneaky here can roam around and get a few pics. You'll be on your way and she'll be happy. You can book that fancy restaurant that you usually break up in...'

Matt leered. 'Yeah, 'Heartbreak Hotel'...'

'...and it will all be good,' said Dan. If he had to hear another cheesy rendition of the Elvis hit, he would have to strangle his friend.

'Sweet mate, I owe you. I'll just go and explain to Lisa.'

Lisa hardly seemed to notice Matt and waved him away airily. Funny, thought Dan, I think Mr Ego has missed his mark with this one. She doesn't seem that into him.

An hour later, Dan decided that he was definitely into Lisa. From the time she slipped effortlessly into a spare pair of overalls, wound her luxurious hair into a spiral and fixed it with one of his carpenter's pencils, he was sold.

'I'll give you that back,' she said. 'I know how you guys are about your pencils.'

Dan roared laughing and Lisa blushed.

'Oh, I didn't mean, oh bother. I'm always doing that. You'd think with three brothers I would have learned by now.'

'So what's the fascination out here with the camera? Most of these cars are junk. I only use them for parts.'

'You'd be surprised. It's all about the angle and the perspective.'

'So, you don't photograph models?'

'Oh *pleease!* I've got better things to do with my time. Models are Matt's thing,' said Lisa. There was a glint in her eye. 'Although I do know a few.'

Dan raised a quizzical eyebrow. This was one intriguing woman. He opened his mouth to ask her to explain, but she moved beside him to show him the photographs she'd taken. Dan was amazed. She'd caught the shine of the mirror reflecting the combination of green paint and orange rust on the old truck at the back of the lot.

'Wow, you have quite an eye. That would look really good on a poster at the front.'

'It's yours,' she said, smiling.

'Well...' said Dan, losing the power of speech, '...stay as long as you like. You're welcome to take as many as you like.'

'Thanks, I'd like that...' Her mobile phone beeped.

'That'll be Matt.'

Dan's heart plummeted.

'Yeah, sure. I'd love to, Matt.' Her face lit up.

For the first time, Dan actually hated his friend. '...so, another perfect date with the wonderful Matt then?'

Lisa laughed.

'Oh, it will be perfect, all right,' she said, 'but not for the "wonderful" Matt.'

'Really?' Dan's voice squeaked. A kernel of hope rose.

Lisa leaned towards him. 'Can you keep a secret, Dan? I mean...are you a really good friend of Dan's?'

'No...well we were at school...but...Oh go on, spill. I'm dying here!'

'Okay. That was the phone call for the 'let me down gently' date at 'Heartbreak Hotel'.'

'You know about that?'

'Oh yeah. Word gets around, especially when your sister was the last one to get the Matt treatment. She was hurt—badly. At least she never mentioned her son, my nephew Damien. Otherwise she'd have thought it was because she was a single mother and blamed herself.'

'You're mighty cheerful for someone who's about to be dumped,' said Dan.

'Oh, dear Dan. *He thinks* he's dumping me, but the girls will all be there.'

'The girls?'

'Yes, all the girls he's used and thrown aside for the last year or so. Most of them are models, like my sister. I met the others at Yoga. They asked me to set him up. I told them I wasn't his type and he wouldn't go for it, but he did. Of course, they had to load me up with make-up the first time and coach me about him. I never thought I'd have to go through with it, but he took to me like a duck to water. I guess I *am* his type. *Female.*'

'Oh, I think you have a bit more going for you than that,' said Dan, leaning towards her.

'You're too kind,' said Lisa, dropping a curtsy, which looked a bit awkward in Dan's overalls. 'The hardest thing has been pretending to be into him. I don't know what anyone sees in him.'

'Really? You know, I think I like you more and more. So Matt isn't your type. Will wonders never cease,' said Dan. 'Well then, what is your type, Miss Conniving Lisa?'

'Oh, I'm beginning to think overalls might come into the equation.' Her smile was shy, but flirty. 'Not prison issue, of course.'

Dan laughed. 'The only 'time' I'd like to do is with you, lovely lady. I would give anything to be a fly on the wall tonight.'

'Then come,' said Lisa, grabbing his forearm.

'Don't you have to stay for the 'break-up'?'

'I don't think breaking up will be on Matt's mind when the other girls walk in, and I walk out.'

Dan laughed. 'So you won't be staying for the main course?'

'Not likely!'

'You'll be famished then...'

'I will.'

'Terrific. I know this great little place...'

I'll be waiting

'Hey Rembrandt!'

Jenna groaned. It was Jack again. Her new neighbour was paying far too much attention to her comings and goings, or at this moment, her backyard activities. She was quietly weeding around the Camellias with her auburn hair tied up. She wiped the sweat that trickled down her neck with the back of her hand – her very grubby hand. She couldn't see him. The man was positively panther-like. Perhaps he'd been a spy in a past life. Maybe if she ignored him, he'd go away.

'Oh, very attractive Jenna,' he purred, his eyes mocking.

Jenna jumped a foot as Jack appeared over the fence. She looked down, and froze as she realised she'd trailed stripes of soil between her breasts.

Why did I wear a bikini top? She wondered. Arrggh. Because I was in the privacy of my own backyard, which has become decidedly less private since Mr Perennial Bachelor moved in next door. I won't let him faze me.

'Thanks for noticing,' Jenna said between gritted teeth.

'You're welcome.'

Jenna continued to pull weeds and turn the soil. He'd soon tire of this.

'You had such a faraway look on your face, Jenna. Were you in another place? Or just wishing?' He leaned negligently on the fence.

Thank God for the fence or he'd probably wander on over, she thought. Maybe I could make it higher.

'I did have a faraway look didn't I? I wasn't wishing, but I am now—for peace and quiet.'

'Ah cruel lips, how dost thy heart beat?' he rambled, throwing himself elegantly on the ground and folding his arms behind his head.

'Shakespeare is rolling over in his grave.'

'I'm not quoting Shakespeare.'

'That's why he's rolling over – crimes against the English language.'

'I'm being original.' Jack smiled.

The man was impossible. He never gave up. He must have an ego the size of the Sahara. The constant parade of gorgeous women to his door had convinced Jenna early on that Jack Nelson was a player. How dare he flirt with her? Bored, that was obviously it. He had introduced himself when he first arrived and given her his business card. The card displayed his profession as a Design Photographer, whatever the hell that was. He certainly seemed to have 'designs' on a lot of leggy, glamorous women.

As much as Jenna wanted to run inside like a sulky teenager, she was determined not to let him get under her skin, or let him know how much he annoyed her. She thrust the fork between the wild violets wondering if she could possibly manage to flick dirt on his pristine white T shirt. That would be easy enough, but making it look accidental would be quite different. Instead she changed the subject.

'You still haven't told me why you call me Rembrandt,' she said.

'Haven't I? Oh, that's easy. I saw your studio.'

'You what? When?'

'The real estate agent showed me through.'

'Where?' she squeaked.

'Oh, everywhere. He must be new. He thought it was your house for sale instead of this place.'

'I'll kill him,' said Jenna straightening up, 'they only have the keys to show tenants the granny flat.'

'Hmm. Oh well, no harm, no foul.'

'That's easy for you to say! It's unprofessional.' She paused. 'You saw my paintings?'

Jenna felt colour rise up her neck to her face. How she hated that. She'd always struggled to hide her emotions, but there they were, written all over her face. Her mother said she could read her like a book.

'They are very good, you know.'

'You shouldn't have seen them. I just...I don't...'

'They are good enough to exhibit. I've been around, you know.'

'Thank you,' said Jenna, biting back the temptation to say 'I'll bet'.

'You really love flowers, don't you? It shows. The colours are vibrant.'

'Oh. Well, I work at a nursery, so I suppose it's true.'

'And you bring your work home with you,' he said, eyeing

her mud-spattered neck.

'Just like you,' she snapped, then felt regret at the withdrawal in his eyes. It was none of her business what he did. He was just being neighbourly.

'Well, then. I'll let you get on with it.'

Jack turned and walked to the house. He didn't know why his new neighbour was so prickly. According to their sparse conversation, usually one-sided, it seemed part of the problem was that she despised his work, which was a bit unreasonable really. A guy had to make a living. And if that living meant glamorous women turning up at his door day and night, why should he explain to Ms Prickly next door. How dare she judge him? He shouldn't care, but he did. Gliding to the kitchen window where he could watch Jenna without her seeing him, he was highly amused to see her banging the shovel against her head.

He laughed. She was human, after all.

One day they might actually have a conversation where he could tell her of his career in journalistic photography. His assignments in Afghanistan, his years of covering disasters, famine, flood and poverty. It irked him enough that his former mates ribbed him over his new career as a commercial photographer. It wasn't his fault that he had only attracted models wanting portfolios. He was stuck with it until his leg healed. In a few weeks he would have the pin and plate removed, where the bullet had shattered his tibia. Maybe then he could get back to serious work. But the specialists had told him not to get his hopes up. At best, his leg would be a long time healing.

The clicking of doggy toenails heralded the arrival of his pug, Nero, tongue hanging to one side. His owner in the kitchen meant one thing. Food. Scratching the mutt's head, Jack obliged.

'You're going to be a problem, Nero,' he said.

Nero wagged his tail, clearly excited to have a conversation with his beloved master.

'What am I going to do with you when I go to hospital? I guess I'll have to ask Debbie, again. I wouldn't dare bother Ms Prickly.'

If Nero heard Jack over the chomping of his meat, he didn't show it.

"Ms Prickly" was well and truly bothered. It was bad enough to miss the two darling neighbours who had become like family. Jean and Arthur Bainbridge moved interstate to be near their children. Jenna kicked herself for hoping for another retired couple, with time on their hands, where she would be welcome without expectation. People she could wander over for a cup of tea, a walk around the garden where she could give advice on their plants, and feel needed.

It was just her luck to get the Playboy of the Year. She groaned as a sleek silver car drove into Jack's driveway. And of course, a gorgeous blonde flew out of the car. How many women did this man have? Although this one was a bit different. No glamour make-up. And a bit frazzled. The woman opened the back door of the car and picked up a pink bundle of softness from the baby seat. Jenna's heart constricted.

When would she stop reacting? She put her head down behind the rose bushes. It wouldn't do to appear to be spying on her new neighbour.

Any minute now Jack would wander outside with that ridiculous walking stick he used. She was sure he didn't need it. He was too bloody cheerful to be in pain. Or maybe one of his paramours had kicked him in the shins. Jenna's face creased in a smile at the thought.

'Excuse me.'

Oh no, she'd been spotted. She wasn't in the mood for conversation with any of Jack's women. She looked up and attempted a smile.

'Sorry to bother you,' said the woman, 'but my brother isn't home. He's usually reliable. I don't have time to wait. Oh sorry, I'm Debbie Waters, Jack's big sister. And don't believe him if he says I boss the life out of him. It's just that he's so annoying about accepting help.'

'Oh,' said Jenna.

'Oh dear, I'm prattling on, I'm sorry,' said Debbie. 'Shsh darling one, I know,' she murmured to the baby, stroking the soft downy head.

'Anyway. I wonder if you could give Jack a message. I seem to have everything in the baby's carry bag but a pen and paper. His appointment for the specialist who's going to remove the pin and plate is at 2.00 this afternoon. He'll need to phone our other sister, Jane, as soon as possible. Teagan has a temperature and I have to take her to the paediatrician. Oh dear, this is too much information. I just don't want him to miss the appointment, which he's likely to do, because he won't ask anyone for help. He can't afford to miss this one. We were worried enough when the bullet shattered his leg bone ... oh blast, I can't remember the name of it. Didn't pass Anatomy. Never mind. Could you just tell him when he gets in that Debbie can't take him and to ring Jane. Or else.'

'Um... er... of course. I've got it. His *non*-bossy sister, Debbie, demands his attendance at the specialist.'

'Ha Ha. I'm going to like you...'

'Jenna. Jenna Slater. I'll pass it on to Jack. I'd shake your hand, but...' Jenna held up grubby hands.

'Ta,' said Debbie, and she was gone.

Jenna smiled. What a lovely woman. Then she remembered that she'd agreed to go to Jack's. Darn.

Jack arrived about five minutes later. Jenna felt a pang of disappointment that she hadn't had time to clean up. Oh dear, what was she thinking? Just because the man was drop dead gorgeous and at least one of his female visitors was a lovely down to earth sister, didn't make Jack a saint.

In her attempt to head him off before he got to the front door, she fell headlong in the rose garden. Looking up, she saw Jack grinning.

'You all right?' he asked, ambling over to her.

Jenna noticed the slight wince in his face as he walked. That was something else she was wrong about. 'I'd help you up, but with this dodgy leg, I'd probably end up on top of you. Going somewhere?'

'Yes, actually,' she said, clambering up inelegantly. 'I was coming to give you a message from your sister, Debbie. She can't take you today because Teagan isn't well, so you have to ring Jane.'

'Good grief, regular blabbermouth, that Debbie. Did she tell you my shoe size?'

'Almost.'

'Blast. Oh well, I'll have to cancel. Debbie must have forgotten that Jane's gone away on business.'

'You can't do that!'

'Not you too!'

'She said it was important.'

'Did she now?'

'Yes, on account of the bullet, and the plates and screws ... and stuff...'

'I wear a size 10.'

'Pardon?'

'Well, it would be a shame to miss out the only detail about me you don't have.'

'You should talk. You prowled around my studio.'

'I did not *prowl*. I never prowl.'

'Well, you can't miss the appointment. I'll take you.' Jenna shocked herself.

She must have shocked Jack too, because he didn't answer.

'I'll come over at 1.00. That should give us time to get to the city. I'll just finish this lot, tidy up and come over and get you.'

Jack hesitated. He could walk to her place, but the thought of having her on his home turf was irresistible.

'Okay. I'll be waiting,' he said.

'Right,' said Jenna, with more conviction than she felt. He'd hesitated. She must have been too pushy.

The afternoon went smoothly. Jack gained a small victory

when he talked Jenna into driving his Lexus, claiming he needed leg room. Jenna remembered the potting mix in her car and agreed. She didn't want to be surrounded by the smell of manure while she was with Jack.

To her surprise, conversation with Jack was easy and relaxed. He told her about his overseas tours as a photo journalist, and she talked about her job at the nursery. She even demurred when he suggested they 'grab a bite' and enjoyed the up-market café he chose. Pushing down the thought that he might take all his women there, she allowed herself to relax.

Several men slapped him on the back, and asked after him. It seemed to Jenna that they were observing her keenly, almost as if it was unusual for Jack to be out with a woman. That didn't seem right, but she couldn't dismiss the fact that his friends were protective towards him.

Over the next few days Jenna was introduced to several of Jack's clients, two who were very pregnant, and to his other sister, Jane. She was very much like Debbie in looks and personality. Working in Human Resources, she was a human dynamo.

Jenna managed to meet them all without going inside Jack's house. He invited her in, but she consistently declined. She resisted being drawn further into his life. Maybe she should spend less time in the garden. She'd never met so many people over the fence in her life.

Jack was nonplussed.

Jenna was friendly and compassionate, but she obviously had some invisible line drawn in the sand. Surely, by now the woman realised his job had integrity. He was becoming more attracted to her, but they were at an impasse. He realised he had his work cut out for him. Even though they conversed with ease, she hadn't ventured even into his back yard.

So it was with surprise and pleasure to find her at his back door, holding a basket of home-grown vegetables. Everything nearly fell apart when Nero licked her leg. She screamed, and would have dropped the basket if Jack hadn't caught it.

'Oh help. Sorry. I'm not fond of dogs.'

Nero, impervious to this indictment on his species, repeated the welcome.

'Erk! Why do they do that? That licking thing?'

'I think it's a doggie hello. I could be wrong, of course. You might just taste great.'

This remark earned him a sharp look. He shrugged.

'Who's going to feed him when you're in hospital?'

'I thought you didn't like dogs. Don't tell me you care!'

'Well, I wouldn't want him to starve. And those sisters of yours are busier than the Prime Minister.'

'And just as capable.'

'That too. I don't know how they do it.'

'Frankly, I don't want to know,' said Jack. 'I'm getting addicted to life in the slow lane. But hey, you can feed Nero for me, if you're offering.'

Of course that gave Jack the perfect opportunity to usher Jenna into the house and show her all of Nero's food and vitamin needs. And if he detoured to his photographic studio, who could blame him. A man had to do what he could.

Jenna was wide-eyed when she saw his work. There were very few glamour shots. And not one nude. Not that she was looking. There was a hint of his former life with a discreet portfolio of overseas photographs, but most of the pictures were of families, gently reposed pregnant women, children at play, and his sisters.

Jack felt unaccustomed warmth at her obvious interest.

'These are wonderful, Jack.'

He had no glib words. 'Thank you,' he said. He didn't take his eyes off her as she wandered around the room, totally at ease, admiration shining in her face. 'Your art is just as wonderful, you know, Rembrandt. I hope you go back to painting.'

Jenna smiled. She'd missed him calling her Rembrandt. 'You don't have any here of your models.'

'What?'

'You know - the glamour models that arrive with cosmetic bags the size of small aircraft.'

Jack laughed. 'You're very observant, Ms Slater.'

His lazy grin unnerved her.

'Well it's a bit hard not to notice when they sometimes trip trap to my door looking for you.'

'Oh I see,' he said. 'And there I was thinking you hadn't noticed my existence. So you thought they were models?'

'Well, aren't they?'

'Not many, as a matter of fact. They're mostly women wanting photos for dating sites.'

'Oh, big market for that is there?'

'Apparently.'

'How are you going to manage work after your op?' Jenna concentrated on one of the family snapshots.

Jack sighed. Rather dramatically, Jenna thought.

'I guess I'll have to hire an assistant for a while.'

'Would I do? I mean it must be hard to get someone short term. I learn fast.'

'Why not. You're not squeamish though, are you?'

'Why?'

'Well, I do videos as well.'

'Oh,' Jenna squeaked.

'Births, sometimes funerals, but labour ward mainly. Would you be okay with that?'

'Sure. Yes, I would.'

Jenna's hands trembled.

I'll be okay, she thought. It's time. It's past time.

Jack moaned. His heart raced. His leg was white hot with pain. There were popping noises, women screaming, men yelling and smoke, so much smoke.

'Oh my God. They're shooting. Get down. Get down. There's a child. The girl. Grab the girl. It's okay. I've got her. I've been hit.'

A damp cloth wiped his forehead. Gentle hands soothed his stubbled chin.

'It's okay, Jack. You're dreaming. It's over.'

Jack's eyes focused on Jenna. Then it came to him. He was in hospital. The operation must be over.

'How did it go? Is my leg okay?'

'Yes. It's just a matter of time now.'

'Debbie. Jane.'

'They've just gone for tea. They'll be back soon.'

Jack writhed, and made a useless attempt to sit.

'Hell. Where is the pain relief?'

'You just have to press this button.'

'I can't. You do it.'

'I don't think I'm ...'

'Just do it.'

'Alright Mr Bossy. Honestly Jack, you're a right sook. I thought you'd been in war zones.'

'Behind the camera, Ms Prickly. I'm not a soldier.'

Jenna smiled at being referred to as Ms Prickly. A few months ago that would have stung, but things had changed, subtly at first. And she was pretty sure he was partly affected by the anaesthetic and drugs. She carefully put the damp face cloth over his face.

'Oi, what'd y'do that for?'

'I plead the fifth. What you don't see won't hurt you.' Jenna pressed his pain relief button, then removed the face cloth. 'You'll have to learn to do this yourself, you know.'

'I've been doing it for hours. I just wanted to see if I could get you to do it.'

'You wretch! If you weren't lying in a hospital bed I'd...'

'What...'

'You'd be lying in a hospital bed.'

Jack chuckled.

The next few weeks passed quickly. Jenna learned that Jack's job entailed a lot more than pandering to vapid women in search of their elusive Romeos. She became so comfortable as his assistant that she began to anticipate his needs before he asked. She would miss this when her long service was up and it was time to return to her job at the nursery.

'Oh Nero! Stop that! Don't lick me. When, and if, I ever decide I want to be licked, you are the last one on my list, Slobber Chops.' Jenna scratched his head, and Nero growled in gratitude.

Jack kept his head down on the other side of the room so Jenna wouldn't see the grin wreathing his face.

The phone shrilled. Jack answered it.

Jenna tried to work things out from the patchy one-sided conversation.

'Oh, I'm so sorry... Of course... No. It's fine... No problem. I'll be there as soon as I can.'

He turned to Jenna.

'It's okay if you're not up for this, Jenna. It's a difficult one. I'll understand. I'll get Deb or Jane if it's too much.'

'If what's too much?'

'One of my clients that I was going to film the birth, is... well, the baby has died. She still has to go through labour. I won't be there for that, of course, but they want photos of them holding their baby. Just still shots.'

'Oh.'

Jenna thought she would faint, as the room swam.

'I've got time to get Deb, she's had kids. You don't have to do it.'

'I'll be fine. Truly.' I can do it, Jenna thought. 'What about you, Jack? You're using crutches. How will you manage?'

'I've got you.'

Jenna thought she'd never known such terror, faced such fear. Keeping busy helped. She made a supreme effort to mask her feelings. She had a job to do. Jack needed her.

Jack came into the birthing suite and spoke softly to the couple, who clung quietly to each other. They were waiting for the sister to bring the baby to them. Jack introduced Jenna. She busied herself, getting Jack's equipment ready and finding a stool for him to sit on. That was easy enough as the nurses gave him an adjustable one. Jenna wondered how the nurses could be so normal at a time like this. Compassionate, but competent.

I'll stand in the background, thought Jenna. I'll be fine. I'll stay back. Way back.

The sister brought the baby in and handed the tiny pink blanket to the mother. Jack snapped continuously as the mother, then the father lovingly cradled their baby. They seemed unaware of Jack's presence. The sister left the room. Gentle tears crept down the mother's face from eyes that were already red-rimmed. The father's shoulders shuddered from time to time. Jack handed him a large handkerchief. The man took it without noticing where it came from.

With an understanding gaze the husband and wife locked eyes. They were ready. Their goodbyes had ben said. The woman glanced at Jenna and held the baby out.

Jenna froze.

'I work in a nursery... oh dear... not that kind... It's okay. I've got her.' Jenna took the baby. Husband and wife melted into each other. Jenna looked around in panic for the nurse.

Then she looked down.

The baby was perfect. Warm and peaceful, her skin showing just a hint of dusky blue. The baby's fingers were curled around the edge of the blanket. Jenna couldn't take her eyes off the tiny infant. With feathery fingers she gentled the baby's cheek. Jack snapped the shutter again and again. Jack held his breath. He understood so much about Jenna now, and yet so little.

With infinite tenderness Jenna kissed the tiny forehead.

'Goodbye, Rose.'

'Her name is Belle,' said a nurse at her side.

'Of course,' said Jenna.

'Don't worry. Are you okay for me to take her now?'

'Yes, of course. I'm not... related...'

But the nurse was gone.

Something in Jack's chest pinged. Oh, he'd had zings and zaps before, but nothing like this. I love her, he thought. I'm falling in love with the value of a woman. For the first time. For the last time. A woman as beautiful on the inside as the outside.

They packed up the equipment and went to the car park in silence. A comfortable silence. Jack's Lexus was an automatic, so he drove.

'I had a stillborn baby,' Jenna said.

'Rose.'

Their eyes connected, with only the dashboard lights to illuminate the distance.

'You did well, you know?'

'I did, didn't I? They didn't allow that when it happened to me... to us. I wish they had. I thought it would be terrible, but it wasn't. Parents need to say goodbye, properly, you know?'

'I think I do. It was almost like having your own goodbye, wasn't it.'

'Yes. A forever goodbye, a proper one. How did you know?'

'I could read it on your face. I'll show you the photos I took when you were holding her.'

'Oh, thank you.'

'You're welcome. Jenna?'

'Yes, Jack.'

'When you're ready ...'

Jenna tilted her head quizzically.

'When you're ready for hello. A forever hello. I'll be waiting.'

Jenna slipped her hand into his, and smiled in the semi-darkness.

The empty book

The pearling light of an extravagant sunrise had scarcely begun to warm the distant hills when he arrived. The man's whose visit I had been dreading. The estranged son of Frieda, the woman I had care for, learned to love, desired to protect.

The cold son who had rejected her earlier attempts at reconciliation, whose silence had pained her deeply. I was biased of course, as her live-in carer and companion, for she had saved me as much as I had saved her.

I had often wondered if his reluctance had anything to do with the lack of an inheritance. Freida had so little to leave behind. She had longed to see him. To ask forgiveness, an act she didn't expect, didn't believe she deserved, so brutal had been her abandonment of him.

Now here he was, long after her death. His overseas commitments, whatever that meant, had held dominion over his chance to grant absolution to his mother. Too late to see how she lived, how survived in her tiny council flat. Here he was, at my home, in my world, where all he would see and possess were her books, and that book. The one where I had written Frieda's story, a loosely collated memoir, where I had hand-written her scattered memories in interview style. 'I left it too late, this story-telling,' she had said, as she struggled to breathe, to remember, as her mind jerked from the war years to her later years and back again.

I had hoped to deal with all of this over the phone, or at least most of it.

However, a brief exchange was all I had been able to achieve. Fragments of that conversation darted through my mind, refusing to take form. I remembered his confirmation of his identity, spelling the names of his parents, his curt request for my address ... and me blustering, speaking into silence.

The metallic screech of side gate startled me.

Hastily pulling on woollen gloves over my medi-burns gloves, I damped down a jab of resentment at his early presence. He wasn't supposed to arrive until the afternoon, giving me time to pack Frieda's things making it easy to hand them over, negating the need for him to enter my home, my sanctuary. I had spent a long, wakeful night rehearsing sentences designed to shorten the visit.

Heavy footsteps crunched steadily on the path leading to the back courtyard.

Bright slanted rays of amber dawn inhibited my view of him as he rounded the corner to the cottage. I shaded my eyes with a hand and saw that he was tall, rangy, male, the species designed to dominate.

Phantom shards of blurred memories sought escape into conscious thought. I fought the too familiar dizziness, then relief, as clarity returned. Frieda had promised I would get better at it 'Try and forget, lieber Ella,' she had said, whenever

I looked like fainting. Which was often in those days. Those days so soon after the fire when PTSD, memories and fear ruled my days and nights.

'You're rather early.' I jabbed the words out, uncaring.

'I apologise,' he said, 'I tried to phone last night.'

'Never mind,' I said, minding very much.

He rubbed his hands together, then blew warm air into them. A normal gesture I found oddly reassuring. I had learned to look for those signs. He held the door open and I stepped inside.

'Shall I?' He moved to shut the door.

'No, don't shut that...' The words spilled onto the slate floor, too hard, too fast. I felt the pulse in my neck stutter a rapid tattoo, and covered it with my hand.

He shrugged and smiled, a casual warm response. I could breathe then. Perhaps he was less dangerous than other men.

The back sitting room was more formal, the reason I had chosen it for a meeting I had done everything to avoid, which hadn't amounted to much in the end.

I prolonged drinking my tea, using the time to restore inner calm, using the practised art of self-talk. Rational steps through the mire of panic. Sometimes, snatches of remembered conversation worked just as well. Breathe in. There is no reason to fear him. Breathe out. You will pack the box, give him the book and papers that constructed his mother's life and he will go. That's all. Not all men are to be feared. Not all.

'You're not what I expected,' I said, instantly regretting the words.

'What did you expect? Someone less Australian?'

'Frankly, yes.'

I gestured for him to sit in the high-backed brocade chair his mother had favoured, and served tea.

'I'm a complete fake, I'm afraid,' he said. 'I know very little German. A little after the war ended, Dad and I migrated to Australia, in '46. We only spoke English at home. My dad didn't want a son to have the disadvantage of a German accent. And call me Luke. I've discarded the Germanic Lukas.'

I flinched, unfairly assuming a further rejection of his mother.

Frieda's books were placed in mute precision on the mantel over the fireplace. My eye caught on the hand bound tapestry one, the pseudo-memoir, but I did not offer it to him. He had given me no clue of his feelings and his abrupt phone conversation still rankled.

He formed a steeple with long tanned fingers and absently regarded the table between us. He could not know I had set out Frieda's tea service after smoothing her favourite lace tablecloth over the polished service of the small round table.

He could honour her, or reject her, as he pleased, but it gave me satisfaction to have the table filled with her things.

I remembered her words: 'This is my Meissen demitasse. It is meine eitelkeit, my vanity, but I do not cherish it for beauty alone, but for the connection to my hometown of Meissen near Dresden in Germany,' she said. 'It's all a little worn now, like me. Come, have tea.'

***

The room was cold. There had been no time to stoke the woodfire. I reached towards the wood-box.

'Let me,' he said.

He chose two pieces of timber and carefully placed them on the open fire, kneeling on one knee to arrange them. He stayed there, semi-crouched, with that strange elegance of men, warming his hands. The timber flared, crackled and hissed as it settled into the embers.

From there, he turned to me. 'Your face is familiar,' he said, his brow creased.

I flinched. I would never become accustomed to the statement. Even Freda had never known, never asked. It was one of the things that made our unlikely friendship so comfortable.

'I can't think why,' I said.

'So, not a reclusive film star? No fortune for revealing your secret hideaway to the masses?'

I shook my head.

'No? Shame.' His smile was crooked. He raised open-palmed hands in a gesture of defeat. A good sign. Humour glinted in his eyes.

'You don't look like a man in need of a fortune.'

'Ah, I am not a man in need of even the desire for a fortune.'

'Which means you are either very rich, or very poor.'

'You forgot "thief", you know, rich man, poor man...'

I laughed. 'You forgot "beggar man".'

He looked directly at me then. His eyes were unusual—gunmetal grey.

Satisfied with the fire, he rose, settled into the chair

opposite me with casual ease. He set about pouring a second cup of tea for himself, asking if I wanted another. I surprised myself by saying, 'Yes. Thank you.'

I remembered Frieda's description of his father.

"He was the kind of man who was at home anywhere, my Heinrich. In others it would have been presumption, but not with Heinrich. He had a way of gazing at you, with intense eyes, catching every word as it fell. People often said his eyes were so dark they were nearly black, but they were grey, like forged metal. Like the man. Fired in steel, and yet, the gentlest man I ever knew. When Lukas was born I boasted about his blue eyes, but Heinrich only laughed. 'All babies have blue eyes,' he said, 'you'll see.' And he was right. Steel grey eyes for meine Lukas."

***

Outside, the sounds of early morning peeled back the day in crisp autumnal layers. The hens were busily feasting on crumbs I had left near the courtyard table. I realised with a shock I hadn't heard the misogynist crowing of King Ralph, the Rhode Island Red. It was an even greater revelation to realise that I was not afraid. "Fear is the thunder of the mind", someone had told me. Probably a therapist, explaining why I didn't hear certain things when I was anxious.

He stood and walked to the French doors. He placed a hand on the pane. The warmth from his breath frosted the glass, as he leaned his dark head against the cool of the windowed panel. A vulnerable gesture.

Then I understood. He was as reluctant as I to venture into

the past. I took the smallest book from the mantel. The hand bound tapestry book.

'She would have wanted you to read it,' I said, nurturing it in my hands.

'How can you know that? Did she speak of me?'

I paused.

'Only once,' I said. It seemed so inadequate.

Grave eyes concurred as he returned to the chair. 'Once,' he said, taking a deep breath. Linking his hands behind his head he leaned back in the brocade chair. The chair where his mother, Frieda had sat when told me the story of her life, of the son I had not known existed. He crossed long lean legs at the ankle. 'Only once. In what—ten years of friendship?'

I nodded.

'If it's any consolation it took her a long time to warm to me. Even longer to open up about … anything really.'

***

'You never ask about my past, lieber,' Frieda had said.

'You never ask about mine.'

'Are we cowards, or ... fools?' she asked.

'I don't know, Frieda.'

Unsure of how to respond I placed a hand on the rheumy swelling of her hands. She had shared so little of her life with me over the past ten years of our friendship, a photo here, a memory there; a sigh, a whisper.

'I think we are fools,' she said.

***

Luke stared at the ceiling. 'I'm sorry. I have no measure for this ... no yardstick for lost mothering,' he said. 'I've felt satisfied, a lie, I know. I have been a man with no family, no anchor. I told myself I felt no loss, and I believed that fiction until you found me. I was not prepared. They say you don't miss what you never had, and that was true for me. It might not be for some, but, my father ... he was enough. He was wonderful.'

'That's exactly how she spoke of him,' I said.

'Then why?'

'The day, when she spoke of you, and your father she gave me this, to write her story. For you.'

'I'm sorry,' he said, 'this is so much to take in. I ... would you do something for me?'

'If I can.'

'Read to me, read the book ... maybe ...'

'It's not written as you would expect. I wrote the conversation as it happened ... to me ... not ...'

'Sounds perfect.'

I read.

***

'Come!' she said.

I pursed my lips and folded my arms.

'Always you react the same way when I say "come". Yes, I am bossy German.' Suddenly her voice was tired. 'You have much patience for an old woman tired with life. Please bring me that book.'

I smiled. 'Shall I read to you, Freda?'

'Not today, lieber.'

'But this one is empty.' I flipped to the middle of the book. There was a sketch of a ship on one page. On another a man and a boy with long coats, bent forward against a cold wind that ruffled their hair as they stared at the horizon. 'It only has sketches. Did you...'

'Yes, for memories without photographs, for what I hoped or perhaps I dreamed.'

She rested her head on the chair-back.

'Today, I want to tell you a story. Of a country at war, where patriotism demanded compromise. Some of us could not, you know.' She dapped her eyes. 'Yes, lieber it is my story.'

'But the book?'

'That is for you to write for me.'

Tears tightened my eyes. Freda handed me a sepia photo of a smiling bride and groom. Gesturing for me to throw a rug over her legs she gazed out of the window for so long I wondered if she had gone to sleep, but when she spoke her voice had changed.

'It was 1935. We were madly in love...'

***

A soft sigh from Luke interrupted.

I picked up the box and reached inside. Sifting through the papers I found a photograph. Luke reached for it with hungry fingers. Then he drew back.

'Luke? Are you okay?'

'I want to ... my hands are sticky ...'

'Oh here.' I handed him a linen serviette.

He looked at the photograph for a long time. 'My mother. It's weird, I'm looking at a stranger. I can't even see myself in her. I should feel something.'

He held the photograph, gestured for me to continue reading and closed his eyes.

***

'There was talk of war, but I didn't care. Heinrich wanted to wait, but I was so young, just sixteen. We married quickly. The young have no patience, lieber. I was living with my brother and his wife and they were glad for me to leave. So extravagantly I loved him. I could not bear to lose him. Our son Lukas was born on Christmas Day that year. Meine Lukas. Heinrich knew war was brewing. The men talked of little else. They believed they could resist the Nazis politically. Avoid war.'

'But he agreed to go to England?'

'He was offered a job at the War Office, as translator. I thought it would be enough for him. I pushed him to choose. I pressured him to leave the country. I could not stay. But I never told him ... I had not the courage ...'

'I don't understand,' I said.

Even then Frieda's eyes were fearful. 'I was a Jew. And worse, I was ashamed of it. I thought Heinrich would think less of me. Jews were so hated, and not just by the Nazis. I was foolish. I should have trusted him. Trusted our love.'

She patted my head. 'I boarded the ship. I was so relieved. I did not doubt that Heinrich would come. That he would be on the ship. I searched, frantic, but they were not on board. So many people everywhere, British, Jews, and Germans, all

209

fearful. It was chaos. Then it was too late. I could not get off the ship. I thought the worst. Heinrich had deserted me. Perhaps he had found out that I was a Jew. I was afraid. On the ship some watched us carefully. Germans were not trusted. I didn't speak unless it was necessary, then I said little. On board that ship I knew everything had changed. Life in London would be impossible for me. Alone with no support. No husband with a prestigious position. I was no longer the wife of Heinrich Richter, with diplomatic connections, no longer the wife of a translator for the War Office. I was no one.'

'Then our ship was bombed and we berthed in Sweden. We were held over there. That is when I met Robert Richards. We met in the queue for meals at the hotel that served as a temporary immigration camp as well as an interim place for dispossessed persons. He was a British Jew—a wealthy businessman with good connections. His wife had died in the bombing. he was on his way to Australia. I was cramped with fear and desperation. I spoke so little English and he spoke German. He was kind and so patient when all I did was cry for my husband and son that I assumed were dead. They must be. Heinrich would never have missed the boat if he was alive.

'Richard was much older, he was 45 and I was only 19. He suggested that I take his wife's papers. Our surnames were similar. The passport photos were grainy. I resembled his dead wife. We swapped the photos and I threw my papers away. I think he loved me, even then. So, I became Caroline Richards, until arriving in Australia, when I reverted to Frieda. I told everyone Frieda was a childhood name, a commonplace thing in those days. We were new, no one asked. Anyway, I lived an isolated life. People thought me aloof. Still do. I didn't care. We lived quietly. Richard didn't seem to mind. We were happy—in our way. I want you to know that. I want my son to know that, meine Lukas. Ask him to forgive me, will you, lieber?'

***

Luke learned forward and put the photo on the table. 'So that's why my father couldn't find her. It was as if she had vanished into thin air. No one with the name of Frieda Richter set foot on English soil. Dad caught a later ship. He'd been held up by a Nazi inspection. He worked, as arranged, as a translator in the War Office in London. He kept searching for some word of her, he had many contacts you see. But there was always the possibility that she had died in the bombing.'

'She wanted me to find you. When I knew your name...'

'Of course.' Tears trailed a silent path down his face. He stared into the garden beyond the small courtyard.

The clock ticked in the background as silence stretched like taut canvas.

'Would you like more tea?' I asked. Leaving the gloves on the side of the armchair, I moved to the small polished table and repeated the tea rituals Freda had taught me.

Lukas moved to sit opposite me at the polished table. He reached for my hand, tracing a raised contorted scar.

I drew back.

'I'm sorry,' he said, 'Did I hurt you, Ella?'

'No, it's not that. They're numb now.'

'But you are not.'

I looked away.

'I know your face.'

The dreaded sentence. The awful apprehension. My gut clenched. I felt faint.

'You are the woman whose husband killed your only child,' he said. 'In a house fire.'

There it was. The truth I had hidden for ten long years.

'And these...' he said, tracing the scars with gentle fingers, 'are marks of courage. Never be ashamed.' He took both my hands in his.

I could not meet his eyes.

'Will you read to me again, Ella?' he asked. 'It's a huge imposition, I know... '

I shook my head.

'It's such a rare pleasure for me. I am so glad you found me. He stood and held out a hand to me. 'I would like to see my mother's grave.'

'Oh, of course, here is the map.'

'*Come.*'